FISHY

DEALS

BENEATH THE SURFACE

By LARRY JARBOE

FISHY DEALS Beneath the Surface is a work of fiction. Names, characters, businesses, organizations, places, events, and incidents either are the product of the author's imagination or are used fictitiously. Any resemblance to actual persons, living or dead, events, or locales is entirely coincidental.

ISBN-13: 978-1466294523
ISBN-10: 1466294523

DEDICATION

This book is dedicated to my son and daughter, John and Jodi. There are no children in this world I would rather call my own. They are the finest examples of what a man or woman might become.

FISHY DEALS: Beneath the Surface

Chapter 1 A Blast from the Past

When the phone rings after midnight, it is usually bad news. Commissioner Jerry Largent had become used to regularly receiving such calls. Jerry was downstairs reading his stack of grant applications, public works agreements, commendations, zoning text amendment requests, and other County government paperwork when the lone phone in his home rang three minutes past the beginning of Tuesday morning.

Commissioner Largent scanned the Caller ID screen. He did not recognize the number. It was not Sam the Snakeman who called from his basement lair in P.G. County to talk about his one man sax playing jam sessions in empty stairwells. No, ninety year old Miss Edna was not having another bout with insomnia. John Herriman's number had not shown up for eight months. His battle with chronic back pain was over. John put a pistol to his head and pulled the trigger in January.

The Area Code was unfamiliar to Jerry. He assumed this call was a misdial. He was wrong.

Following the second ring, Largent picked up the receiver and recited his standard salutation, "Hello, this is Jerry. Can I help you?"

"Buenos dias, Capitan Ronco."

There was only one person in the world who might address Commissioner Largent as Captain Grunt in Spanish.

"Carlos, it has been a long time since we've spoke. Probably, not long enough." Largent dryly quipped.

"Jerry, my friend, I owe you three great favors. Should you not grant me the honor of paying you back at least a little bit of the debt I owe you?" countered Carlos.

In another place and time, young U.S. Coast Guard licensed Capt. Jerry Largent operated a snorkel excursion boat from the Coral Reef Park docks in Key Largo, Florida. During a week's vacation from the Park, Capt. Jerry agreed to navigate the yacht owned by Columbian banana baron Carlos Castaneda through International and Cuban waters.

He knew he was breaking many laws, but he would make enough cash to buy his own party boat for reef fishing. Plus, he would be delivering automatic weapons to Cuban freedom fighters.

A hundred grand for a few days' work on the water was a lot of money back then. Capt. Jerry, the-would-be fisherman, had been hooked. He would not have taken the deal if he had known the trade was not for cash, but cocaine.

And, the deal went terribly wrong.

Under the light of a full moon in a jungle clearing in Cuba, Capt. Jerry shot three Cuban drug runners from the depths of the mangrove underbrush to rescue Carlos in what should have been a one on one transaction.

The first two shots from Jerry's Ruger Mini-14 semi-automatic rifle were clean kills. The initial squeeze of the trigger delivered a head shot. The next quick shot was placed between the back shoulders and through the heart of the second Cuban as he spun around. The third Cuban was hit on the run in the thigh. As he fell, Carlos finished him off with his bare Columbian hands.

Capt. Jerry might have been a naive young man far from his native turf, but he was a good shot.

During the empty handed, high speed run back to the Keys, Carlos opened up to this young man who had saved his life. Carlos told Capt. Jerry about his true enterprises as Columbian drug lord and International hit man. Carlos paid Jerry the money promised and offered him three free hits should he ever need those services.

Jerry walked away with the cash and returned to his day job at the Park. Six months later, he moved north to work in his family sawmill in St. Mary's County, Maryland. His child to be deserved a better place to grow up. The hundred grand made a nice deposit on a waterfront home on the Patuxent River.

That was thirty years ago. Not a day had gone by that Commissioner Largent did not remember that night.

The thick Columbian accent interrupted Jerry's trip down memory lane.

"My friend, you have beeen a very busy leetle Ronco. I have a request to put a hit on you. It seems you are making some very powerful people very nervous." said Carlos.

"Yes, I've sure upset my share of apple carts, but those zoning decisions that I made were based on fairness for all. The Boss Hogs need to play by the same rulebook," said Commissioner Largent.

"Oh no, Capitan Ronco. The hombres who wish you to swim with the fishes are not the local barracudas. These are the big sharks. It is your other activities that threaten their livelihoods. Your life is an easy trade-off." said Carlos.

"But Carlos, who would want me dead other than the local big boys? I don't have a lot of money. Don't have any debt to speak of. I live cheaply. Heck, I even drive a homemade electric car to save fuel," stammered Jerry.

Carlos now adopted a far gentler approach to the conversation. "Jerry, please tell me about your electric car."

"Carlos, ten years ago, I put an electric fork-lift motor into a 1985 Toyota MR-2. A battery bank went in the back trunk and I mounted a gas powered generator under the front hood. It was a plug-in hybrid that I drove around town mostly on battery power and recharged at night. Longer trips which I seldom took required using the generator. I got over a thousand miles per gallon the first year by using mostly electricity." Commissioner Largent matter-of-factly stated.

"Over thousand miles per gallon!" Carlos was incredulous. "What did you do with the car?"

"Well, the kids at our local high school wanted an electric car to race so we dropped the genset and doubled the spiral wound lead acid batteries and voltage. We called it the Green Hornet after the school's mascot. For a couple years, we held the National Electric Drag Racing Association record for fastest high school built car in the United States, but that is old news." Jerry continued. "My latest adaption of the car has a long range lithium battery pack and a generator that runs on water for extended range."

"Jerry, did you say your car runs on water?" Carlos questioned.

"Well, I mostly run it on electricity because it is so quiet and maintenance free, but the water fueled genset does make the long hauls possible." Jerry replied.

Carlos delivered his assessment of Jerry's situation, "Jerry, you are a public official that has a car that runs on water. No wonder they want you dead!"

Then, Carlos directed Commissioner Largent to get a pad and pencil and take his special number. He said that he would not take the contract from the man who called from a yacht called "Gusher" docked in Ocean Reef Country Club. This was the first favor Carlos could pay back by not contracting the hit on his good friend and life saver Capitan Jerry Ronco.

"Jerry, they will soon come after you with someone else. They will not fail. You must disappear," counseled Carlos.

"Carlos, before you go, know that Carla is very well and happy." Jerry said.

"Gracias." Carlos hung up.

As Commissioner Largent shuffled the papers for the public meeting that morning and pondered his fate in his chair beside the phone, he wondered what his constituents might think if they knew the truth about his wife: Commissioner Largent was married to the sister of one of Columbia's most notorious drug dealing hit men.

Chapter 2 Opposites Attract

The August full moon lit up the mouth of Indian Creek in front of the bedroom window in the Largent home that faced upriver toward the small town of Benedict in neighboring Charles County. The moonlight that beamed through the window illuminated Carla's olive colored face as she slept. It was two A.M. Jerry had retired to their bedroom, but he did not go to bed. He sat in the dressing chair and quietly focused on the smile reflected from Carla's lovely Latin lips as she lay dreaming.

Rhythmically, Carla gently pushed little Carlena securely seated in the children's swing at the Gilbert Run Park near the manmade lake. She then joined her daughter in dizzying spins on the playground merry-go-round before helping her little girl take repeated trips down the slide. Her precious child was almost four years old. In Carla and Jerry's joint memory, Carlena had not aged a day in a quarter of a century.

Their only child's timeline on this world ended the day when Carla looked from that same bedroom window to see little Carlena's toy Hot Wheels trike floating in the water in front of their docks.

Carla had only been distracted for a few moments as she searched for a receipt from the Sears surplus store in the pockets of her blue denim jeans crumpled in the clothes hamper. The junior drum set she had purchased for Carlena's upcoming fourth birthday lacked a crash cymbal. The perceptive customer assistant from Sears waiting on the unhooked downstairs phone was the first call in to the Charles County Sheriff's Department when she heard the scream that echoed through the house.

The Charles County dispatcher was coordinating with his St. Mary's counterpart when Carla's breathless call came into the emergency operations center under the old jail beside the circuit courthouse in Leonardtown. She had run to the end of her dock. The Mattel tricycle was bobbing in the water. Carlena was nowhere to be seen.

Carla's frantic call is recorded among the thousands of tragic events stored in the St. Mary's County 911 archives.

Upon orders to go home from Gibbs, the mill accountant, Jerry arrived to see two St. Mary's Deputy cars, a State Police cruiser, the Mechanicsville Volunteer Fire Department truck, and the new Mechanicsville Volunteer Rescue Squad ambulance parked in front of the house.

Little Carlena's lifeless body was found late that evening in a cove of cat-tail reeds up the creek.

In vivid dreams, Carla played, danced, and sang with her daughter. This was her subconscious relief valve from the unremitting guilt she suppressed for that brief distraction from her motherly watch so many years ago. Or, as Carla believed, the dreams were a prelude to the joy they would find when they reunited in the next world.

During the day, Carla Largent was an interpreter at the Charles County Courthouse in LaPlata for the Spanish speaking legal and illegal immigrants who found their way into the Charles County Court system. She quietly sympathized with the hard working laborers guilty of simple misdemeanors who had come so far to find their way behind bars.

But, she had only contempt for the murderers, rapists, and pedophiles who invaded her adopted country from south of the border.

Unfortunately, with the urbanization of that once rural county and the takeover of the one party Democratic entitlement politics from adjoining Prince Georges Country, Charles County had become a mecca for low life criminals of all cultures.

At least, her own brother with his despicable corrupt business enterprises had treated her well. Carlos provided a good home in Miami far from the poverty they had been born into. He paid for an excellent education in a private Catholic girls' school. And, he allowed Carla to date and marry a rather eclectic but honest American who loved her dearly and provided her a more than adequate lifestyle.

How many other orphaned Columbian girls could be so fortunate?

Though she seldom sought to conjure up her poor struggles as a child in South America, during the quiet moments between her busy life in Southern Maryland and the peaceful deep dreams with her departed daughter, Carla often remembered those happy years in South Florida.

When Carlos privately chartered the 49 passenger vessel called the Infante for her twenty-first birthday at Pennekamp Coral Reef State Park in Key Largo, he was actually looking for an ambitious and knowledgeable captain. Carlos could not have foreseen the additional consequences. Carla had no friends to celebrate with her and Carlos did not want to enter the clear waters where the Christ Statue resided in a beautiful coral ravine on the deep side of Key Largo Dry Rocks.

Capt. Jerry volunteered to buddy up with Carla as her snorkeling tour guide over the reef. Jim, his first mate, stood watch onboard and kept Carlos company. In the water, Capt. Jerry was a perfect gentleman and a living shield when a large reef shark swam by, too close for Carla's comfort. Only on the way back to the dock did Capt. Jerry learn that this Carlos Castaneda was the wealthy owner of a banana plantation, not, as Jerry assumed, the author of the book about the Yaqui Indian shaman. Capt. Jerry also discovered that Carlos and Carla were not spouses but siblings. Before she walked off the boat, Capt. Jerry Largent had the phone number to their condominium in South Miami.

Carla was quietly amused when Capt. Jerry arrived in a rusty Keys cruiser in front of her high class coastal condo off Florida Highway A1A. The rag top of the baby blue '63 Ford Falcon convertible had long rotted away. The homemade plywood roof only covered the front seat. The back seat was exposed to the weather that was generally pretty good. Capt. Jerry had drilled holes in the back floorboard for the wet season.

Capt. Jerry had the original Key Largo low rider with a golf cart battery bank packed in his back trunk. The half dozen deep cycle Trojan batteries were the mobile power source for his travel trailer parked in a mangrove clearing at the end of a limestone rock lane on Card Sound Road. Plugged into a shore receptacle near the dock beside the

Marine Patrol boathouse in Pennekamp Park, Jerry's battery bank charged up courtesy of the State of Florida while he ran reef trips.

The rectangular box that extended up from a hole cut in the hood capped out Capt. Jerry's custom mods to his very unconventional car. He had installed a Nay Box, designed by Elmer Nay prior to 1930, that vaporized gasoline to give him better mileage. In the Jimmy Carter years of high fuel prices and even/odd purchase days, a car that could go from the Keys to Miami and back on two gallons of fuel was a big deal even though he was constantly adjusting the contraption. However, Jerry knew he could get better than the seventy miles per gallon he was getting with his crude convertible. His goal was to get a hundred miles per gallon in a hundred dollar pick-up truck. Jimmy Buffett would be proud.

Carla did not drive and did not understand the technical nuances of Jerry's jerry rigs. He made her laugh and showed her a new colorful underwater world. He helped her escape from the dense Miami metropolis, through Cutler Ridge and Homestead, then, either down the 18 Mile Stretch or across the Card Sound Road Bridge (if he had a dollar to spare) to their humble hide-a-way in the mangroves of North Key Largo.

Together, they helped customers on the snorkel boat he worked on. At night, she sold beer and cut up bait for the passengers on the party boat he captained for evening snapper fishing trips from the Holiday Inn docks near Mile Marker 100. His own boat was an old Sears canoe with an electric trolling motor that he used to cruise the mangrove creeks and shoreline. While clad in a Speedo bathing suit, cotton gloves, and snorkel gear, Jerry pulled spiny lobsters from their coral rock lairs in those mangrove creeks for seafood feasts. Carla was the bag lady. She snorkeled with him carrying the dive bag full of lobsters that he harvested.

Much to her dismay, Carlos encouraged their relationship. She was twenty-one and he needed a good captain.

Chapter 3 High Mileage and Open Meetings Act: Little Known Facts

The warm wet wake-up kiss on his forehead was a pleasant introduction to the greater challenge of arising from the dressing chair that he had fallen asleep in. Sharp stabs of pain radiated from the small of his back as Commissioner Largent pushed himself to his feet on slightly shaking legs. Though a time or two he had nodded off during long budget hearings, he was not used to sleeping upright for any extended time.

"So, you prefer the four legs of a chair over my two loving arms." chided Carla as she dressed for her job at the Charles County Courthouse.

"No, nothing like that." mumbled Jerry. He could not disclose his conversation with her brother in the early hours of that morning. Plus, he was two hours behind his own schedule to arrive at the Commissioners table in Leonardtown.

Without a shower or shave, he jumped into his dress pants, donned a short sleeve shirt and tie, slipped on a black pair of nylon socks and his black leather shoes. On the way out the door, he snatched the green sport coat that matched his sporty car. Prior to closing the front door, Commissioner Largent called up the stairs, "Carla, I love you!" for her and the entire neighborhood to hear.

Though he could not see her response, that peaceful smile of hers that so entranced him in the moonlight broke forth for a few moments in the light of day.

It was 8:30 A.M. when Commissioner Largent peeled rubber out of his driveway to make the twenty mile plus run from Golden Beach south to Leonardtown. The lithium batteries in his self-engineered car had a hundred mile range so he had plenty of juice to go to the County Seat and back without having to plug in for a re-charge. The meeting would start at 9 o'clock which meant he would be on time, just barely.

Normally, Commissioner Jerry Largent would arrive two hours early for the weekly County Commissioner meeting. This was his time to organize and, once more, review his paperwork. He also took this quiet time to scan the hundred plus pages of bills that were to be paid by the authorization of the County Commissioners. Regularly, he found bills to be paid by the St. Mary's County Commissioners for hundreds of dollars in beer and liquor receipts at the County owned and operated Canoe Neck Creek Golf Course. Any other county would have privatized the bar and grill long ago but, in the Land of the Fiddle and the Flask, the local elected officials coordinated to keep special perks beyond the public view.

Commissioner Largent's votes against these bills and the padded expense accounts presented by his fellow commissioners did not earn him any favor at the table though he had no problem regularly winning re-election with minimal expense or signage. Everyone knew that Commissioner Largent was a little out there but he always worked to do the right thing for the taxpayers. Plus, the local bigwigs and bureaucrats hated him. Long before the emergence of the Tea Party, Jerry Largent was rocking the boat in St. Mary's County.

As Jerry drove in swift silence south to the meeting, he thought about the bigger boat he had rocked with his little water powered electric car. He knew about the deals that had been cut and the people who had been eliminated to keep the big oil tankers cruising on a steady keel. According to his research, Charles Nelson Pogue's famous 200 m.p.g. carburetor was bought out by Standard Oil Company in the mid-1930's. That device was later used to beat General Rommel when it was secretly installed on Allied tanks and Bren gun carriers during WWII. A tank that gets 35 miles per gallon can roll a lot further before refueling. The Desert Fox was outfoxed when the Allied Forces did not run out of fuel as he had calculated. Instead of shooting sitting ducks, General Rommel found his outnumbered Panzer division the central targets in the North African shooting gallery.

The inventor who made our own CIA aware of the Extra Low Frequency wave bombardment initiated by the Russians on the United States during the Cold War became their target when he discovered a way to crack the water molecule beyond Faraday's Laws of Physics. Andrija Puharich found himself on the run as he drove a water fueled motor home around South America to escape their threats.

Perhaps, Stan Meyer was the most notably publicized person to mysteriously die after building and promoting a vehicle that was fueled by breaking water into combustible hydrogen and oxygen gases. Jerry was familiar with all these stories and many more. He knew Carla's brother was right. "I am now in their crosshairs. It will be only a matter of time before someone is going to squeeze the trigger." he thought to himself.

With this view of his own diminished mortality taking understandable precedence over the weekly administration of local government, Commissioner Largent made it to the table just before the camera started documenting the meeting.

Commissioner President Doris Gunn-Manning called the meeting to order promptly at 9:00 A.M. Her keen sense of personal observation noted Commissioner Largent's second day whisker growth and his unusual lack of promptness. "Something is amiss here," she thought as she opened the meeting and proceeded to follow the agenda according to Robert's Rules of Order.

After Commissioner James Lyons read the weekly prayer and led the Pledge of Allegiance, the St. Mary's County Commissioners proceeded to entertain the business they were elected to do: set policy, oversee administration, and maintain the budget of a growing County in the State of Maryland. Commissioner President Gunn-Manning called for an approval of the bills.

With a motion by Commissioner Kenny Leonard and a second from Commissioner Drake Alvey, the motion proceeded to a vote. The unanimous vote of approval stunned all the Commissioners who expected Largent to vote "NO". Commissioner Leonard even muttered under his breath, "Gotcha Sucker!" Neither the microphone nor the reporter from the *County Sentinel* picked up the quiet exclamation.

Tucked deep in the hundred and nine page listing of expenses were two bills totaling $1,431.72 to pay for liquor and beer at the Canoe Neck Creek Golf Course. Though Commissioner Largent had missed the expenditure, his fellow commissioners intended to imbibe from the public funds later that evening.

The rest of the meeting proceeded smoothly. There were minimal controversial issues as is the usual case in local governments. Commissioner President Gunn-Manning closed the meeting a few minutes before noon. Commissioner Largent thought how much his life had changed in twelve hours. He realized that this might be his last meeting.

He did not realize that the other commissioners were planning to attend their own closed meeting later that evening in Virginia.

Based on State legislative mandate, St. Mary's County has its very own Open Meetings Act which requires that a majority of the elected officials overseeing a board or commission cannot meet without proper public notice. This means that no more than two County Commissioners can legally discuss an issue in private that they might vote upon. In the past, the Old Boy Democrats simply disregarded the law. With the election of Republican candidates like long term incumbent Jerry Largent and newly elected Doris Gunn-Manning, the network of bubbas had to find a way to bring the other side onboard. Unanimous votes do not stir up much public consternation.

They had given up on Commissioner Largent years ago, but Commissioner President Gunn-Manning was an easier touch. Doris Gunn-Manning was the local version of former Alaska Governor Sarah Palin. Like Sarah Palin, Doris was a political figure who cut a striking figure in her black sequin dresses that she wore to all events. She was a beautiful redhead who turned heads and promoted a conservative philosophy. Her bullet shaped campaign signs: "A Gunn-Manning Woman" easily moved people from both sexes and parties to vote for her in this rural county.

Newly elected Commissioner President Gunn-Manning knew about the Open Meetings Act. She refused the initial invitation from Commissioners Leonard, Lyons, and Alvey to meet privately in a backroom at the Canoe Neck Creek Golf course following the weekly publicized meeting to strategize on behalf of the local Boss Hogs. Though unlikely, someone might get wind of this long standing violation of the Open Meetings Act and disrupt her political ambitions beyond the electoral killing fields of local governance.

Commissioner Alvey was probably the craftiest of all the commissioners. He came up with a plan to hold the secret meetings in Virginia. "The St. Mary's Open Meetings Act is a State law that does not apply in Virginia." explained Drake (often called "Duck") to Doris. "We can hold our special meetings in a backroom in Colonial Beach across the Potomac River. It will be all legal and you'll get a heads up on the local Boys who will make sure to pump up your campaign funds for a costly State race."

The combination of money, power, and ruling class status sold her on the deal.

Chapter 4 A Covert Rendezvous

Less than twelve hours since his Columbian brother-in-law, Carlos, thoroughly disrupted Commissioner Jerry Largent's total outlook on life, Commissioner President Doris Gunn-Manning closed the commissioners' formal public meeting prior to noon on Tuesday, August 16.

"I hereby adjourn this meeting of the Board of St. Mary's County Commissioners." she said as she firmly tapped her gavel down.

Commissioner Gunn-Manning looked forward to an afternoon off watching Fox News prior to her non-publicly scheduled meeting later that evening in Colonial Beach on the other side of the Potomac River.

Commissioner Leonard drove straight home for his daily nap. His seniority on the commission was based on his age as all three Democratic commissioners and Commissioner Largent was each serving in their third and final term of office. In their wisdom and understanding of politics in the Maryland Mother County, the State legislators in Annapolis had imposed a three term limit on St. Mary's County local elected representatives. Unfortunately, the State Delegation did not consider such legislation for them.

Commissioners Alvey and Lyons drove to a little Leonardtown restaurant and wine store called Danny Boys Bistro tucked on a backstreet near the old funeral home. Drake and James had secretly bartered a County grant with the Town Council to get a zoning upgrade for the proprietor. A lifetime of free lunches was the reward for their effort.

Commissioner Largent, out of habit, wheeled his little electric sports car back up Route 5 to his mill in Charlotte

Hall near the County Line to finish off the day loading a dry kiln with 8/4 fresh cut poplar lumber destined to be shipped to a furniture factory in China. Jerry grabbed a couple value sandwiches at the nearby Burger King for two dollars plus twelve cents State tax. He did not know that Carla was planning a steak dinner for two that evening for his loud declaration of love earlier that morning.

He plugged his car into an extension cord outside his office trailer and changed into a tee shirt, jeans, and work boots. The old Caterpillar 920 articulated fork lift started easily. Jerry Largent fell into a steady rhythm of stacking packs of lumber into the kiln.

At five o'clock that evening, he rolled the heavy doors shut. A half hour later, the sawdust fuel was generating wood gas that burned to heat the boiler for an affordable, renewable, clean burning heat supply. The thirty thousand board foot lumber charge drying in the kiln would be completed in two weeks.

"Will I be here in two weeks?" he thought to himself as he silently cruised home.

While Jerry was driving home to Golden Beach, Commissioner President Doris Gunn-Manning was being escorted by Commissioner Kenny Leonard in his new Lincoln Town Car over the Rt. 301 Harry Nice Bridge on their way to a covert rendezvous at the Lucky Strike Saloon in Colonial Beach, Virginia. Commissioner Leonard was glad to drive, he was afraid of the water.

Commissioners Drake Alvey and James Lyons had already arrived, by boat.

Duck and James made a point to come early to meet in the back room of the restaurant bar on the Potomac River. They had time to down a few cold 10 ounce Budweiser beers from the boat's cooler and order a couple fried seafood platters before the other attendees would arrive. Mostly, they did not want Doris to witness their mode of transportation across the river. Better they should keep her clueless on the origin of the County maintained cabin cruiser berthed at the Canoe Creek Campground and Marina adjacent to the County run golf course.

"Doris may be in cahoots with us, but she was born elsewhere. She'll never completely come on board. So keep your mouth shut about the boat." said James to Duck.

"Sure Jimbo (James Lyons local nickname) I get it. Don't ask. Don't tell." replied Duck.

The 33 foot long officer's launch that was secured to the end of the dock that evening was secured a couple decades ago by the Seventh District Community Improvement Association to ferry tourists to the first colonial landing site in Maryland, St. Clements Island.

The 7th District C.I.A. purchased the former naval transport vessel at an auction in Norfolk, Virginia for twelve hundred dollars and trucked the boat to a marina in Virginia rather than cross the Rt. 301 Bridge with an over-wide load. The boat was launched and towed across the river to Murphy's Marina which was close to the historic site and newly constructed County museum.

Due to insurance concerns, the improvement association turned the title and registration over to the County Commissioners. The marine transmission leaked a half gallon of oil each way from the old 471 Detroit diesel engine that slowly pushed the vessel to and from the island. The resulting oil slick from the bilge pump was reported by the *County Sentinel* which prompted the then reigning commissioners to close the passenger service for a complete overhaul of the engine and marine gear.

Upon hearing the estimate of twelve thousand dollars to fix the boat, then Commissioner President Billy Arnold declared, "We don't need no navy. We can't afford no navy. We already have the navy at Pax River." referring to the large naval research installation on the other side of the County.

The officer's launch was tied to an abandoned dock up Canoe Creek and forgotten.

During his first year of office, Commissioner Largent got a phone call from the new owner of the old dock to which the boat was still tied.   Neither he nor any of the other commissioners knew the County owned a cabin cruiser.

But, Commissioner Jerry Largent had been a U.S. Coast Guard licensed captain for many years and a pirate for the people. He knew how to save the taxpayers many hundreds of thousands of dollars with the old scow that was in the commissioners' possession.

Chapter 5 the County Yacht

St. Mary's County is traditionally known as the Mother County of Maryland. In 1634, when the first English colonists landed on St. Clements Island just south of the mouth of the Wicomico River, a Potomac tributary, they discovered a fertile land ready to clear and cultivate. The four hundred miles of shoreline around the peninsula were adjacent to waters that were thick with oysters, crabs, and fish.

The local politics of this rural region that was relatively isolated until modern times can easily be traced back to the Civil War. The vast majority of St. Mary's Countians were Southern sympathizers during that divisive period of history. Maryland, however, was a border State with Union troops occupying Baltimore for the entire war, preventing secession. The conservative Democrats in the Mother County considered President Abraham Lincoln to be a despot and a liberal.

Except for a few brief moments since the end of the Civil War, Southern Democrats have controlled the political power structure in St. Mary's County. Commissioner President Doris Gunn-Manning's election over a liberal Democrat proved that the system was going to change to a two-party system with her simple message of support for the Second Amendment overriding education, public safety, and growth issues.

The long term support for fellow Republican Commissioner Jerry Largent came from neither the

Republican nor Democratic political elite. They all hated his guts.

He drove quietly around the County in his little water powered electric hybrid car helping people become self-sufficient rather than dependent on government subsidy. Jerry also found efficiencies in government and voted against entitlement funding for special interest groups. When he voted against tax increases while providing a reasoned alternative fiscal plan, both the liberals and the Democratic power mongers howled in protest. This only earned him more votes with his common sense constituents who dominated the voter registration list.

That said, Commissioner Jerry Largent could not help but push the limits of his authority from time to time to save hard earned tax dollars. "There's more than one way to skin a catfish!" was his favorite saying.

The modifications to the officer's launch berthed at the Canoe Creek Campground and Marina were fabricated according to Jerry's recommendations.

Soon after his first election, Commissioner Largent attended a public hearing hosted by the Maryland Department of Natural Resources to dredge Dukehart's Creek. The cost which was to be shared by property owners along the creek was well over a million dollars. There were not enough property owners to spread out the price to reasonable limits. Having just discovered that the St. Mary's County Commissioners possessed the big single screw launch, Commissioner Largent asked the State officials, "Is prop dredging legal to open up the channel?"

The State officials said prop dredging was illegal.

Then Commissioner Largent asked, "What if I put a big boat on a squat plane and troll a bucktail behind, then I am fishing, correct?" The State officials scratched their heads and agreed.

The small crowd of frustrated waterfront property owners cheered.

After work, Commissioner Largent and a couple fishing buddies from Public Works cleaned out the boat which had filled with rainwater but was still afloat due to naval buoyancy specifications. They scrounged parts from local marinas that were glad to help provide a reasonably priced solution to expensive DNR and Army Corps of Engineers dredge projects. A bigger and heavier pitch prop was installed. The little worn out, water logged 471 Detroit diesel engine and transmission needed to be replaced with some real turning and churning power.

The 500 kilowatt 1292 Detroit diesel generator used by the Office of Emergency Management for back-up power was due for scheduled replacement though the unit only had fifteen hundred hours on it. The little four banger diesel could not compare with twelve cylinders of turbocharged power from the 1292. It took a lot of creative fiberglass work and a marine transmission from a small tug that was being scrapped in New Jersey, but the replacement Detroit diesel was eased into the hull at Murphy's Marina.

The sea trials were impressive to say the least. At 1,300 r.p.m., the bow of the launch rose up and the propeller dug down over four feet to the bottom. The soft sand and mud was easily blown away. Hard objects like submerged logs or discarded engine blocks were deflected by the full two inch thick skeg that ran from the end of the keel to connect below the prop.

At 2,250 r.p.m., that old officer's launch cruised at almost thirty knots!

Once a month, Commissioner Largent and a motley varied crew of County fishermen boarded the boat for a fishing trip. From three hours past high tide to almost slack low tide, they "trolled" back and forth at 1300 r.p.m. through a scheduled list of creeks keeping the way clear for fellow boaters. There was always a bucktail trolled behind but they never caught a fish until the one afternoon they snagged a Mud Shad stunned from the commotion.

That Mud Shad is mounted in the Commissioners' Meeting room in the Senator Paul Bailey Building. They also got a picture posted in the *County Sentinel* to prove they really were actively involved in fish sampling, not prop dredging.

The taxpayers were pretty happy with this arrangement. After the initial costs of retro-fitting the boat which tallied up to a couple thousand bucks and a lot of donated time and materials, the cost of fuel was free. Those smart Public Works employees built a waste oil filtering vat to recycle used restaurant fryer vegetable oil which helped boost State mandated recycling statistics. The filtered fryer oil powered the boat instead of expensive diesel fuel. Commissioner Largent built a big trucking style hydrogen booster to help combust that thick fuel mix and clean up the emissions. The Canoe Creek Campground and Marina provided dockage for free while the local marinas maintained the boat at no cost to the County.

A two grand investment was saving the taxpayers millions.

However, while Commissioner Jerry Largent had one purpose for the retro-fitted officer's launch named "Bottom's Up", Commissioners Drake Alvey and James Lyons figured another use for the vessel to help them continue to tap the taxpayers.

Chapter 6 Ten Ounce Buds and Bubbas

"The ten ounce Budweiser beer has been the choice beverage of St. Mary's County residents for over half a century," Commissioner Kenny Leonard explained to Commissioner Doris Gunn-Manning as they crossed the Governor Harry Nice Bridge into Virginia. Commissioner Leonard knew little about our Nation's history but he had driven a beer delivery truck for forty years. Kenny knew his stuff when it came to cold brew.

"Sometime back in the mid-Fifties when Elvis was just starting to raise a ruckus, a few dozen cases of ten ounce Buds from Texas were shipped in to Dean and Son Distributing to fill out the normal order of twelve once cans. The delivery man at the time decided to drop off the cases to the small Seventh District bars where he figured the bartenders and patrons would be too inebriated to notice the lesser volume." explained Commissioner Leonard as he continued his story:

"However, the customers immediately howled in protest. A drinking man knows when his drink is short. The bar owners discounted the brew by fifty percent to clear the shelves. Then, the local boys developed a taste for the beer which stayed cold through the last swig. Before long, people were actually willing to pay as much or more for a ten ounce Bud than a twelve ounce Bud. Go figure."

While the two St. Mary's County Commissioners were still making their way to Colonial Beach for their secret meeting, Buster Butler was wheeling his big black Cadillac Escalade into the parking lot of the Lucky Strike Saloon. Buster was a big black man who was also held the distinction of being the richest resident of the Mother County.

Busta Butt, as he was called by his friends and enemies, owned two major cash cows, Butler's Oil Company and Busta's Beef n' Pork Bar-B-Que. Despite his huge gruff appearance, he was a remarkably charming man. He also was an extremely talented singer, well versed in all music genres. Though he could easily belt out the most soulful gospel verse, he particularly enjoyed wowing the predominately white County residents with classic country renditions. No local boy or gal could harbor resentment against a black man who could sing "He Stopped Loving Her Today" even better than George Jones.

Butler Oil Company was founded by Buster's father who was the son of a former slave and tenant tobacco farmer. Butler Oil was not noted for gouging customers or unethical business practices. He had a contract with County government that was break even at best. Butler Oil Co. Inc. helped legitimize the actions of Busta's barbeque outlets.

Buster Butler had portable barbeque grills positioned at major County crossroads adjacent to public parking lots. Though he owned land for other purposes, his trailerable barbeque stands were in the public right-of-ways. He did not have to purchase properly zoned land or even pay property tax on his very popular outdoor eating establishments.

Though he occasionally, for the IRS and Health Department records, purchased USDA inspected pork, most of Buster's gutted pigs were bought directly from the local Amish and Mennonite farmers who were glad to have a direct market for their hog farms. All the beef he bought was USDA inspected but Mister Busta added another type of meat into his "sliced meaty beef" sandwich.

Somewhere about the time that ten ounce cans of Bud beer were gaining popularity, the St. Mary's County Commissioners decided to import whitetail deer to replace the virtually depleted native stock. As long as tobacco was the prevailing crop there was not too much problem. Deer have better sense than people when it comes to consumption of this toxic weed. However, over the past decade with farmers grabbing Tobacco Buyout free government money and growing corn and soybeans instead, the deer population surged. Well fed does regularly produced two fat fawns a year.

Buster Butler solved the deer infestation problem for the frustrated farmers. He paid twenty bucks for every gutted fresh deer carcass, regardless of season, and sent his refrigerated delivery truck directly to the farmer's house to make the pickup.

In his own barn on the tenant farm that his grandfather had labored and his father bought, Busta had a major meat processing and cooking operation. The pig, beef, and deer carcasses were cooked on slow turning spits over wood fired coals. The low priced, cooked and sliced venison was blended in with the beef and soaked in Busta's secret sweet barbeque sauce which he also sold by the bottle from the stands and in local stores. No one could tell the difference between the beef or venison or cared. People lined up at his outlets for pulled pork or sliced meaty beef sandwich. The taste of Busta's Barbeque was addictive.

For an extra twenty dollar bill neatly folded and slipped into the transaction, a small sugar packet containing another substance was dropped into the paper bag with the napkins and sandwich. Each barbeque trailer was also a crack cocaine carry-out. Busta Butt was the biggest drug dealer south of Washington D.C.

Buster Butler was not meeting with four out of five of the St. Mary's County Commissioners in the backroom of the Lucky Strike Saloon in Colonial Beach that evening to discuss his oil company or his lucrative barbeque outlets. He had discovered an even better way to make big bucks with very little effort. In his shirt pocket, Busta carried a list of zoning changes that he wanted to be made.

Chapter 7 Let's Make a Deal

"A governmental office complex zoning makes no sense at the northern end of St. Mary's County," explained Buster Butler to Commissioner President Doris Gunn-Manning who listened in rapt attention mesmerized by Buster's magnetic personality.   Commissioners Drake Alvey and James Lyons nodded their heads in a Budweiser induced stupor while Commissioner Kenny Leonard grabbed left over hush puppies from their plates.

"There are people starving in India." announced Commissioner Leonard as he cleaned his fellow commissioners' plates.

"That large parcel presently zoned as Governmental Office Complex north of the County transfer station should be rezoned as General Commercial along the highway to match the properties on either side of it. The back hundred acres should be designated Heavy Industrial to encourage new manufacturing jobs to make America stronger."   Buster Butler knew how to flip the right switches on his conservative patsy named Doris.

What Buster did not tell the new Commissioner President was that he had a twenty year fixed price option on the property. He secured the exclusive option for a hundred thousand dollars from Widow Alice Somerville who thought a million dollars was a lot of money for a two hundred acre farm at the edge of a sleepy town.   When her husband died in 1989, this was the largest farm owned and worked by a black family in St. Mary's County.

Unfortunately, none of their three sons shared their father John Somerville's work ethic raising tobacco after he was not there to goad them to work the farm each day. All three sons consistently reside in the County jail for drug dealing. However, none have done time in the State prison system as the local judges and States Attorney also have a close ear to Buster Butler and his simple requests to assist the black community in St. Mary's County.

The two Somerville daughters were very good at caring for their mother but lacked the managerial skills to operate a large farm. They were not able to collect the Tobacco Buyout money that started flowing in 1999. The Somerville's had stopped farming Type 32 Maryland tobacco too early to collect that form of agrarian welfare most of the local white farmers were cashing in on. Buster Butler's offer ten years ago was a Godsend after the County government had zoned their land for Governmental Complex use thus rendering it virtually non-salable.

What the Somerville ladies did not know was Buster's behind the scenes pick on the Planning Commission, Thelma Goodrich, convinced her fellow board members to create such a zoning category during the Comprehensive Plan Zoning Review in 1996. Mrs. Goodrich made a logical case hinged on the need to provide important infrastructure for North County residents, but the actual outcome was to crush market competition for the property so Butler's offer would look good. That was two Comp Plans ago.

Now, Buster Butler needed to get the property rezoned back to a reasonable designation to cash in on the big bucks. The front commercial parcel was contracted to be sold to WalMart for ten million dollars while the back industrial lot had a six million dollar sales contact to host a natural gas electric generating plant to take advantage of the new gas line being buried along Rt 5. Both deals were contingent on specific zoning approvals.

"A fifteen million dollar profit is not a bad deal for a little foresight and political manipulation." Buster thought and then remembered his other overhead. "Well, knock out a few thousand in campaign contributions to the bubbas and this new bimbo, but it is money well spent. This zoning business is a lot less aggravating than hustling fuel and keeping the barbeque outlets cracking. This is the easiest money I ever made. If I didn't like my samwiches so much, I'd close the pits." Busta especially liked stopping at almost any busy intersection in St. Mary's to grab one of his pulled pork sandwiches. He avoided the meaty beef combo. For Busta Butt, there was always a free lunch.

From his home on the Patuxent River, Commissioner Jerry Largent was obviously not aware of this legislative liaison occurring across the Potomac River. After a delicious steak dinner cooked by Carla with a bottle of Sweet Walter red wine for dessert, he and his lovely Latin wife retired to their bedroom for a liaison of their own.

The peaceful smile returned to Carla's moonlight face as she slept beneath the crumpled covers but Jerry was not able to fall asleep beside her.

Jerry Largent silently eased out of his driveway in his unique sports car running in electric mode a few minutes after eleven p.m. At the same time, Commissioner Alvey cast off the lines connecting the County owned officers launch "Bottoms Up" from the pier connected to the Lucky Strike Saloon in Colonial Beach, Virginia.

Commissioners Alvey and Lyons stayed almost two hours after the other two commissioners and Buster had departed the meeting. Seated in their folding deck chairs on board, they had finished three-quarters of the case of ten ounce Budweiser beer. The cooler would be empty by the time Commissioner James Lyons sloppily pulled the vessel into its berth at the Canoe Neck Campground and Marina.

Drake and James did not know that they had a designated driver who was waiting for them at the dock. Ginny Lyons had arrived to make sure that her husband, James, got a safe ride home. Normally, she would not care if he got caught driving drunk because the *County Sentinel* did not report such events. However, Ginny had accidentally stumbled on to dwihitparade.com while cruising the Internet that evening.

"My boy, Jimbo, may be a lame duck in Leonardtown but he can run for another office. If he gets caught drunk and exposed on that scandalous web site, he'll be a dead duck. I want to be the First Lady of a State Senator not a local yokel's frumpy wife," thought Ginny as she imagined fine dinners in Old Town Annapolis from the front seat of her new Toyota Camry idling in the marina parking lot.

As Drake and Jimbo were cruising back to the Seventh District with the throaty diesel loudly resonating in the night across the Potomac River, Jerry was quietly cruising on Rt. 236 wondering what the future might hold for him but knowing what he must do next.

He pulled into a gravel lane and stopped at a public phone booth located in a very rural setting. Public pay phones have become largely a thing of the past with the common use of cell phones. However, Rt. 236 curves through the heart of Amish Country in Southern Maryland. Though most Amish sects prohibit ownership of telephones, they do not prohibit usage of telephones. Pay phones are a very popular commodity in Amish communities. This late in the evening, Jerry Largent had the phone to himself.

Less than twenty-four hours since the call from his notorious brother-in-law, Jerry dialed the number that Carlos had given him from a phone booth surrounded by a field of contracted burley tobacco that was ready to be harvested. The Amish farmers refuse to accept government subsidy to stop farming their tobacco.

"Capitan Ronco, we do not speak for thirty years and now we converse twice in less than a day! What do I owe this privilege to speak with such an esteemed public official?" Carlos said upon answering his old cell phone that was manufactured before 911 tracking hardware was required by law.

"Cut the baloney, Carlos." Jerry replied. It had been a very long day. Jerry was not about to embark on either pleasantries or satirical debate.

"First, Carlos, thanks for the heads up about the contract on my life. As far as I am concerned, we are even. But, if you want to make things really right, send a check for a thousand bucks a month to Carla from one of your legitimate business enterprises after I disappear or am bumped off, whichever happens first. The house is paid off. She deserves a little extra cash to enjoy her retirement in a few years but not enough to subsidize a boy toy to replace me." Commissioner Largent flatly stated.

Carlos could not help but smile as he realized just how practical and sensible his American brother-in-law had become. "Yes, my brother Jerry, Carla will be taken care of but only just enough."

"Then we are done," said Jerry as he hung up the phone.

"Maybe not." thought Carlos. He flipped his antiquated Timeport digital/analog cell phone shut as a new day began on the East Coast.

At 8:30 A.M., Commissioner Alvey's nephew, a grounds keeper at the neighboring Canoe Creek County Golf Course, quietly pulled his electric golf cart into the marina and stopped beside the "Bottom's up" tied in her slip. He reached over the starboard side and hoisted the empty cooler over the rail to refill for the St. Mary's County Commissioners meeting next week.

Chapter 8 How a Water Car Works

By 9:00 A.M. on the day after the St. Mary's Commissioners meeting, Jerry Largent was busy at work in his full-time job driving a Caterpillar 920 forklift to unload a charge of lumber from the second dry kiln of the three kilns on his family lumberyard.   He had already made a second run into Amish Country since his phone call before midnight to Carlos. This time, he had taken his quiet car on Rt. 236 to pick up Levi, an Amish man who subcontracted his band mill business for custom sawing.

Part of the deal with Levi to operate his one man mill on the lumberyard was that he would have a ride to work. Levi did not need to have his horse hitched up all day. The short diversion from his own commute did not bother Jerry.   He appreciated the simple life Levi and his community lived.

"Looks like Tom is going to be Levi's full-time driver." Jerry thought as he planned for his departure or demise depending on what the next few days might bring.

Jerry pulled the 920 up to the office trailer and walked inside to talk with his business partner. "Tom, I've got to make a run down County. Will you cover me for the day?"

"Of course, Jerry, but I'll be gone on Friday if you can return the favor." replied Tom.

Jerry agreed and hoped he'd be able to follow through.

After unplugging his MR2, Jerry pulled off his sunroof and tucked it behind the driver's seat. He sat down and popped between two contacts on his dash a small plastic black box about the size of a deck of pinochle playing cards. Then, he pushed the two spring loaded buttons that primed and cranked his water fueled generator tucked under the custom built hood of his mostly electric car.

The first button he pushed with his left hand energized Jerry's electrolyzer. This unit cracked a stoichiometric mix of hydrogen and oxygen from distilled water that he used to fuel his genset. Also, it started a small fog producing machine that he bought on eBay. The pond fogger made cold water vapor. The hydrogen/oxygen/cold vapor mix was ready to feed when Jerry's right hand pushed the second button a few seconds later. That button was wired to the starter solenoid.

Vroom! The ten horsepower Briggs & Stratton engine easily cranked. Jerry released pressure on the buttons while the over-ride circuit kept the electrolyzer and fogger running thus producing the clean fuel that was now powering the engine to generate electricity. The water fueled gen-set powered his car beyond the hundred mile range of its lithium batteries.

Commissioner Jerry Largent was ready to roll down County.

The five kilo-watt generator produced a steady hum as Jerry eased his hydrogen on demand hybrid car off the gravel mill road to head South on Route 5 which is also known as Three Notch Road. This is the main arterial spine that runs down St. Mary's County. The Three Notch Trail was used long before Commissioner Largent cruised his non-polluting vehicle down that corridor. The native Indians carved three notches on tree trunks along this long trail for sign markers.

Though the Maryland Indians had no means of transportation beyond poplar log canoes and their own two feet, like all of us, they too produced carbon emissions from both ends of their alimentary canals. However, the water powered Green Hornet MR2 rolling down the Three Notch Trail only produced warm water vapor as exhaust. This clean burning, cheaply fueled car could easily change the history of the world. Why would someone want Commissioner Largent dead?

In New Market, Jerry wheeled his car right again on to Rt. 236 to cut across the County to head south on Rt. 234 to go to one of the last refuges of rural character left in St. Mary's County, the Seventh District.

He turned left on Rt. 234 and passed the Maryland International Raceway drag strip that is well known to the world drag racing community and is often featured on the television show "Pinks". The Green Hornet got its first national media exposure in a Washington Post article about electric drag racing and the work of the high school engineering club. At the test trials graciously hosted by the owner of the track, the Post reporter caught a great picture of the car smoking tires at the starting line. The picture was not published. Electric cars are not supposed to smoke tires.

His electric car was not breaking any NEDRA (National Electric Drag Racing Association) speed records as the entrance to MIR faded in his rear view mirror. Running just below the speed limit, Jerry wished to keep a low profile which was hard to do with the big hood scoop in front of him and the yellow lightning bolt emblazoned on each side of his car.

Despite his best intentions, Jerry could not help but take three quick laps in the Chaptico round-a-bout before shooting off to Rt. 238. There was no traffic on Rt. 234 that time of the morning and Commissioner Largent was both notorious and re-elected for pushing the limits of authority to put power back in the people's hands.

Though not pushing beyond the speed limit, he and his car were breaking other limits, the known laws of physics.

Technically speaking, a water fueled vehicle is a waste of time and effort because it takes more energy to break the bonds of H_2O than is derived from combusting the hydrogen fuel with oxygen. Combine that with engine efficiency losses and the concussive nature of perfectly mixed hydrogen and oxygen gas, most engineers will tell you that a water car is totally impractical if not impossible.

But Jerry Largent did not have a degree in engineering; he was simply able to figure out how to get things done.

The power of his hydrogen on demand electric hybrid sports car did not start with the engine that was air cooled by the custom scoop on the hood of his car.

The 50 watt solar panel mounted over the rear engine hood was the starting point for Jerry's water fueled hybrid vehicle.

This panel converted free energy of the sun into electrons that charged a single deep cycle 12 volt battery. This battery not only cranked the Briggs & Stratton generator engine. It also powered a step down transformer that delivered six volts to the three cell electrolyzer that Jerry had built using a modified design of the rig that Archie Blue had used to power his water fueled car in New Zealand over thirty years ago.

Jerry had compensated for the faster flame speed of the hydrogen/oxygen mix he was using by mechanically moving the small engine timing past top dead center with a 2-1 sprocket and chain assembly to another magneto that energized the coil to the spark plug. This design also eliminated the potentially disastrous waste spark that would be shifted to the intake stroke with such a timing change on a small 4 cycle engine. The water vapor introduced into the air stream cushioned the concussive hydrogen explosion that might otherwise shatter the engine in a short while.

With all these technical aspects resolved, there is one major problem. Such a basic hydrogen and oxygen generator will not produce enough fuel from water to run even a small engine for more than a few minutes.

However, Jerry had wired a second circuit into his simple hydrogen cracking unit. This assembly pulsated high voltage electricity through the small plastic box that Jerry had earlier inserted into his dashboard. The little black box clipped between the two leads contained the secret of how he could turn water into an efficient fuel to power an internal combustion engine cheaply and cleanly without polluting the environment.

As he cruised through peaceful low country farms of the Seventh District to his first destination, Commissioner Jerry Largent tapped the magic black box and thought to himself, "No way would I sell the secret of this simple circuit to be placed on a black shelf and forgotten.

Everyone in the world deserves to benefit from this knowledge."

No wonder someone wanted Jerry Largent dead.

Chapter 9 A New Newspaper

"Hi Punkin," Commissioner Largent said as he slowed his car to a stop beside Punkin Nelson in the parking lot of the White Neck Creek Bar and Marina in the Seventh District.

Punkin and her husband Bardog Nelson owned the family business that Bardog inherited from his father who built the drinking establishment and docks during the Depression. Hardly anyone actually knew their real names. Their nicknames had stuck since childhood.

Punkin Nelson was a short plump woman with an exuberant personality while her husband of forty years was a lean grizzled man covered in leathery skin who had a big, somewhat ugly head like the oyster toad fish that is locally known as the Bar Dog. Long before he owned the bar, young Nelson had been dubbed Bardog.

"Dee by Gawd, Cap'n! What brings you down to the Seventh in this heat?" said Punkin.

Jerry opened the car door and gave her a hug but left his generator running under the hood to catch up the charge in the batteries that had been lost during the trip. His car consumed more energy that the genset could keep up with but he always found time to talk with the people he had been chosen to represent. The little water powered hybrid electric car might not fit most folks' busy schedule but it matched Commissioner Largent's personality quite well.

The batteries would get a good recharge. He was somewhat long winded.

In the cool of the bar, Jerry initially turned down Bardog's offer of a cold ten ounce Budweiser beer. He had never drunk an alcoholic beverage in public since his first election but he realized he was not likely to complete this term. So, he relented.

"Just one," Jerry said.

As he savored the ice cold bite of the Bud, he asked Punkin, "Is the County still busting your chops over the overnight accommodations?"

"No, we hired an out of County attorney who did a little homework and sent a letter to the County Attorney documenting the legality of our use versus the illegality of the Canoe Creek Campground and Marina beside the County Golf Course," said Punkin. "I guess they didn't want to grab that tar baby."

"Funny, that letter didn't make it over to the Commissioners' mail log. *The County Sentinel* might have picked up on the irony." Commissioner Largent noted.

"*The County Sentinel* wouldn't recognize a story if it whapped 'em upside the head!" said Punkin. "I'm putting out a new newspaper with real news for local folks."

"What!" said Jerry? "You're going to go head to head with the *Sentinel.*"

"No way, Jerry, I may be short but I am heads above the boys in the Sentimentell. Who's got more scoop on more poop than the wife of a bar owner?" exclaimed Punkin. "The first issue comes out Saturday."

Commissioner Largent scratched the back of his head as Bardog Nelson quietly threw his voice to Jerry's ear on the other side of Punkin.

"She's just going through her change. She'll come to her senses later."

Jerry hoped Bardog was wrong. A tell all sheet would be good for the County.

He paid for his beer, hugged Punkin and saluted Bardog goodbye. Jerry walked out the bar door and returned to the bright morning sunlight of the parking lot at the mouth of White Neck Creek that flows into the Potomac River. Jerry knew these creeks adjacent to the Potomac River well. They were part of his scheduled prop dredging fishing expeditions on the County yacht "Bottoms Up".

Commissioner Largent also knew that the Nelson Family had saved many lives with their overnight campground beside the parking lot established by Bardog's father after he built the bar. Capt. Sam would not let a patron drive home in a drunken stupor. After the second drink, he took a patron's keys before he would dispense more alcohol to that person.

Both Capt. Sam and his wife, Lily, were adept at determining whether or not a customer was able to safely drive home. Their keys were not available to those who were impaired but Lily made sure they had access to the back seat of their car to sleep off their intoxication. On chilly nights, she made sure that the drunken consumer had a pillow and clean quilt and was tucked in properly. There were even a few cots in the storage room for the coldest of evenings.

A free morning cup of hot coffee was also part of the deal when the customer awoke.

None of the other drinking establishments had such a stringent sobriety requirement. The White Neck Creek Bar and Restaurant stayed busy because the tough watermen who at times drank to oblivion appreciated the gentle feminine kindness and soft touch that Lily provided to make sure of their safety. Other travelers who might have had to share the road with those incapacitated drivers benefited as well.

Only once did anyone make a lewd advance toward Lily.

Back in 1943, Pistol Pilkerton, a full-time farmer and part-time waterman noted for his bad temperament and disregard for private oyster ground boundaries, proceeded to get stinking drunk at the bar. He had been shunned by the local single women who made fun of him for taking advantage of a farm deferment to avoid the draft. When Lily reached across him in his beat up farm truck to tuck his drunken carcass under the quilt on a cool spring night, Pistol grabbed Mrs. Nelson and hung on. Her screams from the parking lot brought Capt. Sam out of the bar with a chair leg that he used as an enforcement tool.

Pistol was whipped with a club to the head.

Before daybreak that morning, Pistol and his Ford truck disappeared. No one really cared.

As Commissioner Largent drove south to Leonardtown, he remembered the story of how Pistol Pilkerton and his old truck disappeared one night. The Potomac River is a pretty broad and deep hiding place for a Model T pick-up and drunken driver. Capt. Sam's pile driving barge could have provided the ride to Pistol's final parking spot that night.

Or, not.

That day was done.

The water fueled generator hummed a steady tune while Jerry wondered what method a professional assassin would take to keep the public spotlight of the media, including Punkin Nelson's new newspaper, diverted from thoroughly investigating his untimely death. Would he be shot outright or might there be a sophisticated chain of events to make his death look accidental or even natural?

He remembered in dismay the events he witnessed on television as a boy surrounding the death of President John F. Kennedy. Why did Jack Ruby kill the one man, Lee Harvey Oswald, who could disclose additional details of the plot? As years passed, Jerry Largent did his homework. He was convinced that the greatest conspiracy of modern times had occurred during the Kennedy assassination and cover-up.

Quite a few years later, President Clinton's Commerce Secretary Ron Brown conveniently crashed into a mountain following the suspicious suicide of Vince Foster.

If the powers that be can pull off such high profile eradications, Jerry realized that he was doomed. Carlos, his friendly international drug dealing hit man and brother-in-law, had given him good advice.

Above Leonardtown, he merged back on to Route 5 which is also called History Highway. In his super energy efficient Toyota, Commissioner Largent mumbled to himself as he passed the Chevy dealership on the other side of the dual lane road, "It's time to get out of Dodge."

Chapter 10 A Plan to Survive

Normally, Commissioner Jerry Largent would have made a left hand turn from History Highway to make a stop at the mega-governmental complex that was housed just east of Leonardtown.

Located there are two courthouses, circuit and district, an eight hundred prisoner capacity jail and a fully covered parking lot for two hundred Sheriff's deputy cars, seventy-four County busses and more than a thousand County employees' vehicles.

Almost all of County Government has been consolidated to this one location and surrounded with wire mesh fencing topped with razor wire.

Within the gated complex are a myriad of edifices, offices, and agencies. The Sen. Paul Bailey Building houses the Offices of County Administration. Public Works and Building Services are disseminated from the Elmer Jarboe Building. Human Services are dispensed from the William Arnold Building. The Sheriff's Department and Emergency Services Complex has not been named as the present Sheriff, Chuck Hall, continues to insist that his name be emblazoned over his domain. The County Commissioners, however, have a continuing resolution that a County owned building, room, park, road, or bus bench may only be named for an individual after he or she is deceased.

"I'd be lucky if they'd name a commode for me after my demise!" thought Commissioner Largent who laughed as he, instead, took a right hand turn into the old town of Leonardtown.

When Rt. 5 was diverted around Leonardtown twenty years ago, the town lost much of the traffic and resulting business. The decision of an all Democratic Board in 1999 to move the historic circuit court function and all other related offices to a consolidated governmental center outside of Leonardtown sealed the town's fate.   The widespread disgruntlement over such a bad business decision was probably the fundamental reason why the Republican Party initially gained a foothold with the election of underdog Jerry Largent in the 2000 Election.

The town has yet to recover. Jerry passed by many boarded buildings on Main Street. He took a right hand turn at the lone intersection and drove past the only two thriving businesses, Dukes Funeral Home and the adjacent Danny Boys Bistro who depends upon the walk in lunch and dinner traffic generated by dead County residents. The liquor license is the key to Danny Boy's success. In St. Mary's County, vast quantities of alcohol are consumed by mourners and celebrants, both of whom will be found leaving a funeral home.

Commissioner Largent wondered if there would be more people crying or cheering at his viewing. Shaking off such morbid thought, Jerry rolled down the steep hill below the now empty courthouse to the Leonardtown wharf. The old bar and restaurant on the pier over Breton Bay Run had burned to the water years ago and never been rebuilt.

A lone fisherman cast his line among the old pilings. As Jerry watched from his stopped car with the generator still running, the old timer's rod bent double. At first, Jerry assumed the fisherman had hooked a snag, but he soon realized the man was fighting a monster.

Skillfully, the seasoned fisherman worked his catch over to and up into the shallows of the old boat ramp that was still used infrequently. Jerry left the car to help the angler but the old man needed no assistance. He eased the two foot long narrow fish with a mouth full of sharp teeth onto the shore.

"Third damned snakehead fish I've caught this summer!" the old man exclaimed. "But, those oriental imports taste real good. Tonight, I'll be eating fresh Chinese fish filets. Sure beats being struck by a Chinese bullet." The fisherman pulled up his tee shirt to show a bullet scar just below his rib cage.

"That one hurt real bad but it was my ticket out of Korea." the veteran stated.

Commissioner Largent thanked the man for his service to our Country and returned to his car.

A tear rolled down his eye as Commissioner Largent rolled south out of town.

This often happened when he visited the Veterans Home in Charlotte Hall or participated in Veterans and Memorial Day ceremonies. Though he had not done a tour of duty in the U.S armed forces, the battle scarred angler had triggered memories of another place and time, specifically, his last moments in a prop driven bomber plunging to the ground, which Jerry could not explain.

He was not afraid to fly but he made his peace with God at the beginning of every take-off. Deep within his psyche, Jerry knew instinctively and inherently when a big plane leaves the ground the options of crash survival are virtually non-existent.

Maybe, his odds were better on the ground confronting a hired gun but who was behind the contract?

"Does the C.I.A. or F.B.I. have a silent mission to snuff out citizens guilty of disrupting the energy non-policy that our Country is suffering from today?" Jerry wondered to himself as he zipped under the thirty million dollar concrete pedestrian overpass at St. Mary's College. "Or, do the people who want me dead come from a far more insidious network?"

Jerry decided the answers to those questions lay too deep beneath the surface for him to fathom as he looked out across the Chesapeake Bay and the mouth of the Potomac River. By land, he could go no further south. In the Point Lookout State Park parking lot far behind him, the little water fueled generator continued to hum pumping fresh, almost free energy into his hybrid electric car's battery bank. In front of him, two great estuaries flowed to the sea.

Beyond the shallow sand bar below the point of land, hundreds of round crab pot floats bobbed in the waves. Jerry imagined they were, instead, the heads of a horde of seals awaiting his departure to land on the beach. The humid Southeast breeze filled his lungs with salt air.

In the depths of his desperate desire for self-preservation and divine inspiration, a plan arose.

Chapter 11 Self-assisted Suicide

With a fresh charge to both his spirit and his battery pack, Commissioner Largent headed up County.

Ridge is the last town before Route 5 ends in the Chesapeake Bay. Commissioner Largent again passed through this thriving town center that depends on fishing, boating, and water sports for economic stability. Thirty years ago, despite widespread public outcry, the State of Maryland installed a massive sewage treatment plant at Point Lookout Park that was and continues to be capable of handling major development all the way up Route 235 to the Patuxent River Naval Base.

Recognizing the potential for an economic windfall, the conservative Democratic County Commissioners of that time rezoned this rural stretch of land as a Techno-Suburban Corridor.

The TSC zoning category does allow relatively high density (half acre lots) but only single family housing is allowed. The success of encouraging large single family home growth below the base was not realized until the BRAC decision of 1994 that consolidated the Warminster and Crystal City Naval facilities to Pax River.

Most of the families who moved to St. Mary's County settled south of the base for the five thousand top paying engineering jobs that had been relocated to the Pax River Naval Research Air Station. This had the benefit of keeping traffic under relative control on the more congested portion of Route 235 north of the navy base. Also, the new well-paying jobs created a huge windfall for the commissioners due to increased income tax receipts and high assessments imposed upon many big homes hastily erected on small lots.

However, the commissioners had one major problem. Most of these higher level civil servants, naval contractors and contract employees who moved from Pennsylvania and Virginia were registered Republicans.

In Ridge, Commissioner Largent hung a right hand turn on Route 235 and took the ten mile trip up through the Techno-Suburban Corridor. Half million dollar homes on half acre lots lined the road and extended east to the Chesapeake Bay where multi-million dollar mansions overlooked private beaches.

Rather than lowering taxes for their constituents, the Democratic Board raised taxes in 1999 to pay for construction of FDR Boulevard neighborhood connector road to offset traffic congestion that might be generated from future Base Realignment and Closure recommendations. Commissioner Largent knew the real reason was to develop a second layer of development of Section 8, low income housing apartment complexes north of the navy base parallel to the High-Tech Highway. The Democratic Board was able to import an off-setting number of Democratic voters who could not afford to live in the more affluent, Republican controlled Calvert County on the other side of the Patuxent River.

Their move also insured that the jail would be filled to capacity and property taxes kept at high levels to support their political aspirations.

Commissioner Largent would not miss the local political subterfuges that occurred in County Government and contemplated his means of evading the impending death by international hit man that Carlos had warned him of.

"It is hard to kill someone who is already dead." Jerry Largent thought as his car was stopped at one of the many traffic lights where this portion of Route 235 known as High-Tech Highway bordered the Pax River Base. "I'll just kill myself before they can kill me."

Jerry smiled at the simple madness of his plan:

A weighted man's body might easily disappear into the deep waters of the Patuxent River that flow beneath the Thomas Johnson Bridge. In late August, the migratory blue crabs feed heavily and can easily consume a cadaver in a week or two.

As Jerry passed through the intersection at Route 4 which connects St. Mary's to Calvert County via the highly arching Thomas Johnson Bridge, he calculated his time schedule.

"Today is Wednesday. Traffic on the bridge is likely to be least on Monday morning between 2 A.M. and 4 A.M. I must be prepared by Sunday to leave this world around 3 A.M. before sunrise of the next day." Jerry nonchalantly said to himself and hoped he would be ahead of his contracted executioner. The old aluminum fifteen foot long Sears canoe that he had bought years ago for seventy-five dollars at a Key Largo yard sale was a key to the success of his suicide attempt and his survival. The canoe was covered in honey suckle vines behind a weathered storage trailer beside an old abandoned mill at his business. The vessel had never been registered and was long forgotten by everyone but Jerry Largent. It would still be watertight and seaworthy.

His business partner, Tom, was taking an extended three day weekend trip starting on Friday so Jerry would not be seen pulling the canoe from its leafy hideaway.

Launching the canoe from the bed of his pick-up truck in a floppy straw hat and dark sunglasses from a nearby boat ramp, he would like any other resident taking an affordable weekend paddling adventure when he slid the canoe into the Patuxent River from one of the many nearby public canoe/kayak ramps on Sunday afternoon.

The boat, paddle, and floating seat cushion would be hidden among the cat-tail reeds not far from the base of the bridge before he drove his pick-up truck back to the mill where he kept it.

His little sports car with the motor still running on water fuel would be found on the shoulder of the road at the bottom of the bridge. A suicide note explaining his duress would be left on the dashboard with a simple will leaving all he owned to Carla except for the remarkably energy efficient car. The signed title in the visor for the modified MR2 would be made out to Ralph Nader. Who better than Mr. Nader might be trusted to stand up for American consumers?

To insure his car was not tampered with, Commissioner Largent intended to e-mail prior to his departure the schematic and assembly instructions for his revolutionary H2O cracking device directly to both Ralph Nader and Punkin Nelson for public distribution in her newspaper.

A small chip of concrete block on the passenger floorboard and manila rope fibers on the passenger seat along with Largent's two well-worn Pirates of the Caribbean Croc sandals found abandoned at the top of the bridge would lead investigators to an obvious conclusion.

While searchers combed the river for his body by day, former Commissioner Jerry Largent and his canoe would be far up a wooded creek hidden in the brush. There, in the cool shade, he planned to rest and await the cover of darkness and the outgoing tide to carry his still breathing body in his low profile vessel steadily paddling to a quiet anonymous life down the Bay and beyond.

Chapter 12   Diego Garcia

Before turning off the ignition switch of his water fueled generator that was still charging his hybrid electric sports car parked in his driveway, Commissioner Jerry Largent checked the trip indicator on the odometer.

That day, he had driven over 123 miles on a little more than two gallons of distilled water.

Jerry Largent knew that water is not technically a fuel.

The conventional science of our generation recognizes that more energy is needed to break the hydrogen and oxygen bonds than can be gained from igniting the resulting gas mix.

Jerry, however, shared the success of other water car drivers like Archie Blue, Andrija Puharich, Stan Meyers, and Herman Anderson who had discovered how to extract and apply a tiny fraction of limitless free energy that is available throughout time and space.

Properly channeled into the electrolytic circuit, this additional energy produces an anomaly where the hydrogen and oxygen bonds between the water molecules disappear leaving free hydrogen and oxygen atoms in a temporarily polarized state.

Not only could the dual circuit electrolyzer built by Largent produce large amounts of hydrogen fuel using free energy, the monatomic hydrogen atoms delivered far more punch than traditional bottled H2.

As effective and innovative as his invention was the price of distilled water to fuel the generator on long runs was higher than the price of electricity for the majority of his shorter battery powered trips. The 123 mile trip he had taken that day cost him over two bucks in distilled water while the electric bill to travel that far would have been about twenty-five cents cheaper.

Better range from his batteries would have helped Commissioner Largent to save a quarter and his life. International hit men are not generally offered contracts on folks who drive purely electric vehicles.

Jerry plugged his hybrid into the outdoor pole lamp that he modified as a charging station at his home in Golden Beach and walked in to hug his wife. Carla was preparing for Jerry to grill dinner on the back deck that overlooked Indian Creek.

On her way home from the Charles County Courthouse in LaPlata, she had picked up a dozen fresh ears of silver queen sweet corn at the Amish farmers market beside the North End Library on Route 6.

The shucked ears of corn were wrapped in aluminum foil. Marinated catfish filets were also wrapped in foil with sliced onions and peppers to simmer on the outdoor grill.

Jerry caught those cats Monday evening up Indian Creek from his aluminum skiff powered by an electric trolling motor. So much had changed in just two days.

Though Carla was the queen of her kitchen, Jerry was king in official command of the barbeque grill. The same electrolyzer unit that fueled the generator in his car was installed in a former propane tank connected to fuel the gas grill. This was his first prototype hydrogen gas generator. It was plugged into a standard AC outlet and converted to DC to energize the hydrogen producing cells.

Jerry placed wet hickory chips in the depression of the soapstone flame bed to impart a smoky flavor to the food. Otherwise, the hydrogen fuel would burn too cleanly for traditional barbeque style cooking. Unlike charcoal briquettes, the hydrogen gas flame quickly and evenly distributed the heat to cook their dinner. In less than a half hour, the steaming fillets and hot ears of corn were on the table.

After a simple quiet supper, Carla and Jerry retired to the living room to watch television. Jerry wanted to tell Carla about the conversation with her brother and the events that might soon unfold but he could not.

Instead, he asked, "Are you familiar with Diego Garcia?" "Who is Diego Garcia?" Carla asked back.

"The question should be where is Diego Garcia." Jerry replied.

"Yesterday, Admiral Heinz delivered a presentation to the County Commissioners on the State of the Patuxent River Naval Air Station. During his slide show, I recognized the naval installations on both the East and West Coasts. Out in the Indian Ocean, there was a place in the middle of nowhere called Diego Garcia. I quickly Google searched it and discovered that Diego Garcia is a military base on a coral atoll. I guess you can learn something every day. Like that!" Jerry pointed to the T.V. set.

There, in front of Carla and Jerry, were the words Diego Garcia referring to the same base on a computer screen in a television show.

Carla was astounded but Jerry took the amazing co-incidence in stride.

"That is God whapping us upside the head reminding us that everything has a plan and a purpose. We are fortunate to have witnessed this together. Those unbelievable co-incidental moments are precious gifts to strengthen our faith that there really is a God. And, She does have a sense of humor." said Jerry.

Carla smiled. She could only agree with her husband.

Chapter 13
A Violation of the Bird Flu Treaty

Carla retired to bed around ten P.M. Jerry wandered through the house taking inventory on what he might carry with him in the lone back pack that he was preparing to outfit.

The garage supplied the most provisions.

A filet knife and sheath with sharpening stone were the first items that went into the pack. Jerry loaded a small clear plastic case with fishing hooks, small sinkers, swivels, and a few of the most effective lures he owned. Into the pack, the mini-tackle box went.

On one of the shelves in the garage, there was a brand new rod that almost entirely folded into its handle.

It was a Christmas present from Carla that he had never used. His old one piece rods had far better action but this rig was the right combination for his present circumstances.

He screwed a small Gold Penn spinning reel loaded with 12 pound test line on the reel seat of the compact rod. "Thank you, Carla." he said quietly to himself and put the little rod and reel combo into his back pack.

Below the shelves, in a wooden box underneath a pile of rags was a grey plastic case that Carla was not aware of. Jerry silently slid that gun case into his back pack. Inside was an unregistered stainless steel Ruger P-89 pistol with three full fifteen round clips. Jerry had secured the handgun by trading the mini-14 Ruger rifle he had used to kill the three gun dealing drug runners in Cuba three decades ago.

The 9 mm pistol was somewhat bulky but it might come in handy in a future survival situation. Carla had a twelve gauge double barrel shotgun and a box of double ought buckshot in their bedroom for her protection that she was well familiar with.

Jerry put the partially filled back pack under a ragged tarp and also retired to a well-earned sleep. He would have to find time tomorrow to collect a few clothes before Carla came home from work.

He awoke ahead of Carla and started the day as he would on any Thursday morning.

A cup of coffee was his only breakfast. Jerry walked outside, unplugged his fully charged car, and strapped an open plastic cooler onto the rear trunk of the hybrid sports car with bungee cords to hold Levi's chain saw and tool box.

After delivering Levi to his mill, Jerry started his forklift and proceeded with his daily routine in the real working world. He threw a small pair of needle grip-lock jaw pliers into his back pocket for his back pack inventory and checked behind the storage shed to make sure that old Sears canoe was still buried under the honey suckle. Yes, it was still there.

He left for lunch a little early to throw some jeans, tee shirts, a flannel shirt, a couple towels, toothbrush, a bar of soap, and a disposable razor along with the lock jaw pliers into his, now, nearly full back pack. He screwed the lid on an almost full jar of change that was sitting on his dresser and threw it in which filled up the pack.

Jerry wrapped the pack in an old blanket and stuffed it in a heavy duty plastic garbage bag that he tied, wrapped and placed back under the tarp.

Nothing that Jerry had taken would be missed after his disappearance.

He slapped some peanut butter and grape jelly on wheat bread for his lunch, grabbed a Gatorade from the fridge and headed back to work in his car.

The afternoon went slowly. Jerry tried to rehearse and revise his plan better but the combination of worry and fatigue was setting in. He went through the motions of a typical hot day at work, took Levi home and showed up at his place in Golden Beach only to go straight to bed without a shower.

Intuitively, Carla knew something was wrong when she saw Jerry spread across the top of their bed sleeping soundly at dinner time. She did not wake him but resolved to spend some time with Jerry on the weekend to find out what was bothering him.

Jerry was still in a deep sleep on top of the covers when Carla was ready to go to bed at ten P.M. She gently placed a clean sheet over his body and crawled under the covers on what was left of her side of the bed. His distinct body odor from a summer's day of mill labor assured her that she had married an honest, hardworking man. In a few moment's she, too, was in deep sleep playing with her daughter, Carlena, as Jerry also relived happier times in his dreams.

At two A.M. under the light of an almost full moon beginning to wane, Jung Fang eased his silent electric motorcycle in front of the Green Hornet hydrogen on demand hybrid car that was parked in front of the Largent home.

His real name was not Jung Fang though this alias fit his character much better. Jung was a full-time assassin on the payroll of the Chinese Government. He had an almost unlimited expense account. However, he was quite frugal with his expenses that were purchased under his real name, Arthur Ching. Arthur lived an extremely mobile life in an old camper trailer towed by a used Toyota Tacoma truck. The new state of the art electric motorcycle with sixty miles of range on its lithium batteries was his one major extravagance.

His silent off-the-shelf stealth vehicle also helped Jung Fang attain the status of Number One International Hit Man on a fraction of the budget James Bond 007 might command.

The hasty orders to snuff out St. Mary's County Commissioner Jerry Largent and his water assisted car had come full circle from an unusual source. In her monthly communications with her acupuncture teacher in Beijing, Bluebird Tennyson, a resident of the nearby aging hippies' commune included a clipping from the *County Sentinel* about Commissioner Largent's car to him. The article was slanted to show the impracticality of such a vehicle. The Chinese guru of acupuncture recognized the greater significance and passed the article to a friend in the government information office.

In China, the Office of Information does not exist solely to disseminate information. The primary role is to collect information.

The clipping worked its way through various agencies till the Party officer tasked with oversight of the Red and Green Societies read the translated version. Carl Tse Hung was outraged at this violation of the Bird Flu agreement with the Council of 33 that had been negotiated three years ago.

The Chinese had intercepted information confirming that the Council was preparing to introduce a more virulent version of the Bird Flu into the Chinese population. Enough vaccine had been developed to protect populations of the Western Hemisphere and most of Europe but it was predicted that over two-thirds of the Chinese population would perish. Africa, Russia, India, and the Middle East would also suffer extreme casualties.

The intensely manipulated media coverage of the Bird Flu was a smokescreen for the greater debacle to come.

The Chinese response to this documented disclosure was calculated beyond the Western thought process. The Chinese representative reminded the Council that the Chinese Government knew all of the ten thousand elite members of the Council that pulled the strings of all allied Caucasian governments (except Russia). The Chinese Red and Green Societies claim six million covert members who distribute all aspects of Chinese dominion.

Should the engineered version of the Bird Flu escape from its test tube enclosure, each one of the ten thousand Caucasian elite will be assassinated by professional operatives.

A full folder of information exists on each member in the Chinese Office of Information. The membership Red and Green Societies in China remains a secret.

To pay the price for their projected plan to de-populate China, the Council is required destroy the value of the American dollar and the Euro over a four year period.

The wars in the Middle East must be maintained with an escalation of troop involvement rather than withdrawal.

The price of fuel will be increased on an annual basis to keep the world economy in turmoil while the Chinese are the only people allowed to develop real new energy technologies.

All Bird Flu vaccine currently developed must be shipped by refrigerated container to be warehoused in Central China. No more will be processed.

Should the Council default on these obligations, Council members will be methodically eliminated.

Chapter 14 An Assassin's Assassin

In the moonlit driveway, Jung Fang quietly went to work to booby trap Commissioner Largent's hydrogen on demand hybrid electric car. The driver side door opened easily. Jerry had not locked it.

Jung eased into the driver's seat and reviewed the interior.

There was no overhead light to turn off. The electrical system was as basic as possible. The car had been set up for drag racing so weight had been cut to a minimum. There was not a radio, air conditioner, or heater in the car.

The wires from the ignition key had been cut when the aluminum racing dash was installed. A series of mostly unlabeled switches was installed in the dash. Jung's challenge was to find the main ignition switch.

When Jerry Largent flipped the main ignition switch, electricity from the battery would energize the detonator imbedded in the wad of C-4 plastic explosive planted behind the dashboard in front of the steering wheel. The resulting blast into Largent's chest would kill him while the incendiary charges in the front and rear trunks would create a flaming inferno destroying the internationally sensitive technology under the front hood.

Jung was lithe enough to ease under the dash with his little LED headlamp strapped to his head. The main ignition switch was the first switch on the left as logic would dictate. With his volt meter, he determined which wire was hot. Before he wired the plastic explosive to a wire run from the open side of the switch, he had to satisfy his own curiosity.

He had done his research on the Largent water car. The black box still clipped into the dash was a temptation to great for Jung to resist. He could not remove and pocket it, that would disrupt the chain of events, but he could at least check out the secret circuit within. Only four screws held the cover in place.

Jung unscrewed the four Phillips head style machine screws with a mini-screwdriver. He gently eased off the cover. Instead of capacitors, resistors, or a solid-state timing circuit, there was no circuit. The leads from either end stopped leaving a gap between.

"Damned American trickster!" Jung thought to himself and continued. "No wonder Largent left the car unlocked. He put an empty counterfeit black box in place of the real one. I am glad to be the one chosen to blow him to hell."

Quickly, Jung replaced the cover, tripped the front and back trunk lid latches, hooked up the wire to the C-4 charge and eased out the driver door.

The incendiary packs were pre-fabricated to ignite with a DC surge and gradually build into a flaming fireball. Jung laid one pack over the lithium batteries in the rear trunk. He clipped the alligator clip on one lead to the main ignition wire while he grounded the other wire out of the pack by clipping to part of the car's frame. Quietly, Jung closed the rear trunk.

The other pack was laid over the politically volatile water fueled generator in the front trunk. The two wires were hooked up in a similar manner but Jung slid four big water bottles full of gasoline around the generator and electrolyzer unit to ensure a complete meltdown of equipment that must not be replicated.

He eased away from the car, straddled his electric motorcycle and silently cruised far up the street to watch the show from a safe distance.

Underneath the cover of a broad low Japanese Maple tree at the edge of the hill overlooking the Golden Beach community, Arthur Ching closed his eyes and directed his consciousness into deep meditation. In three hours, the alarm would arouse him.

Chapter 15
Commissioner's Car Goes Kaboom

Fast Freddy Fernandez was not the first choice of the Council's consultant to deal with the Bird Flu treaty violation that St. Mary's County Commissioner Jerry Largent presented with his public display of a water fueled vehicle by an elected official in the United States. Gus Herald had originally tried to contract a Columbian named Carlos who had a far better reputation for professional executions.

Inexplicably, Carlos had refused the million dollar offer. Gus hired Fast Freddy within a day but Fast Freddy took his time driving up from Ft. Lauderdale to complete the mission. He would have flown if this was a simple hit. A car bombing, however, requires explosives that are too difficult to smuggle aboard a commercial airline.

It was almost four A.M. on Friday morning August 19, 2011 when Fast Freddy Fernandez parked his rental car down the street and around the corner from the Largent home.

A half hour prior, Commissioner Jerry Largent had awaken from his off schedule night's sleep and taken an early morning shower upstairs. Jerry Largent was sitting in Carla's unlit kitchen dressed for a day of mill work.

Jerry peacefully contemplated his planned suicide from the Thomas Johnson Bridge and personal resurrection via Sears canoe. He was drinking a cup of coffee and looking out over the moonlit river when Fast Freddy pulled on the handle of the MR2 sports car in the driveway on the other side of his house. The car door was still unlocked.

Freddy smiled at how easy his mark had made his job. He threw the satchel loaded with C-4 plastic explosive onto the passenger seat and quickly dropped into the driver seat.

With a small magnum flashlight, Freddy scanned the dash to find the main ignition lead to wire in the bomb.

To his chagrin, the original key switch wires had been cut. The series of switches across the dash were not labeled.

He flipped the far switch to the right and the passenger headlight arose and moved up and down without turning on.

Fast Freddy quickly flipped that switch off with the headlight back down. He assumed the next switch over was the other headlight but did not know the reason for such a wiring arrangement.

Unlike Jung Fang, Fast Freddy had not done his homework Googling the history of the Green Hornet MR2. If he had, he would have known that the lights were wired by the high school students to wink during parades or wobble up and down opposite to each other while returning to the pits after a successful quarter mile drag run.

Fast Freddy only wanted to make sure the car and Commissioner Jerry Largent became history when he flipped the switch on the far left side looking for the main ignition.

He got half his wish as the C-4 planted by Jung Fang behind the dash detonated and blew a hole through Fast Freddy's chest instantly killing him. The plastic explosive in Freddy's satchel did not detonate but would add more fuel to the growing inferno from the incendiary packs that was consuming the car from both ends.

The huge explosion rocked the Largent home. Jerry was first to see the burning car from downstairs. Soon after, Carla looked in horror from their bedroom window.

For a brief moment, they both saw a silhouette of a man in the flames before fire consumed the entire vehicle.

Carla fumbled for her cell phone to call 911 while Jerry finished the last swig of coffee, set the empty cup in the sink, and eased into the garage. He reached under the tarp, picked up the plastic bag containing his back pack, and shuffled out the back door to arrive at the deep end of his dock.

Jerry slipped off his work boots, tied the two pairs of laces together with a square knot, and hung them from behind his neck and over his shoulders. He reached into the dock locker and grabbed an old dive mask, snorkel, and fins. Quickly, he slipped on the fins, adjusted the mask on his face and eased into the warm water with the buoyant bag.

He was tempted to hide in darkness under the dock and watch the show but he knew daybreak was not long in coming. He pushed the bag ahead of him and started swimming up Indian Creek. Fortunately, there was a strong incoming tide to assist him.

Jung Fang had been roused from his meditation earlier than he expected. He wondered why Commissioner Largent might have deviated from his schedule but was satisfied with the outcome of his own sabotage.

The glowing fireball down the street and the incoming fire truck siren howls gave him a great sense of satisfaction. He hopped on the electric motorcycle and headed out of

Golden Beach to ramp the bike up on the bed of his Tacoma truck parked not far from Jerry's mill in a public parking lot.

He would be leaving the Water World Campground on the Virginia side of the Potomac River that day. He had a list of ten well known public figures much more important than Commissioner Jerry Largent that he must make an example of for his Chinese masters.

Chapter 16 Big Brother Knows Best

Nearly all the residents of Golden Beach had become aware of the burning car on Shoreview Drive. The dark grey, almost black, floating trash bag being pushed up Indian Creek cove by a low profile snorkeler in the darkness had been seen by no one.

Far to the right of him, he passed the pocket of cattails that had cradled his daughter Carlena's lifeless body so long ago. In another place and time, he might have paused in quiet respect but Jerry Largent remained focused on making his way before dawn to the unpopulated stretch of Indian Creek beyond the last houses at the end of the cove.

As the sun was pushing a few rays of sunshine into the Eastern horizon, Jerry hit the mouth of the main feeder creek. He was pulled though by the channeled incoming tide. He would have made a clean escape but for one precocious early rising four year old boy who spotted Jerry from his bedroom window that overlooked the creek. "Mommy! There's a man swimming in the creek with a big bag." Little Tommy Jones called down the hall to his parents' bedroom.

"Yes, Tommy, he is going to feed the walrus you saw yesterday swimming in the creek," explained his mother who rolled over to catch a few more minutes rest. By the time little Tommy Jones returned to his viewing window, the man was gone. The moving tide had carried Jerry around the bend behind the wall of high swamp grass to his left and the wooded wildlife management area in Charles County on his right.

Jerry knew he was not likely to be seen in this section of creek by either a homeowner or boater but there would be helicopters from competing Washington DC news stations that would soon be circling overhead.

As the light of day grew brighter, Jerry slid off his fins and walked across the clay mud shoreline to enter the forest that bordered Indian Creek on the Charles County side. He dragged the plastic bag behind him to destroy his foot prints.

Underneath the thick canopy of an old white oak tree deep in the woods, he would spend the rest of his day swatting deer flies, assessing what had happened, and formulating Plan B.

Life was not nearly so peaceful on Shoreview Drive that morning.

Four volunteer fire trucks from Mechanicsville, Hughesville, Benedict, and the Golden Beach Sub-Station lined the street with three volunteer rescue units. The Hughesville EMS unit had already carried Carla Largent to LaPlata Memorial Hospital in a state of shock. There was no one else for the units to respond to.

Twenty-two Sheriff's Deputy and seven State Police cruisers were on scene with two State Fire Marshalls who had cordoned off the burned cinder of a car that had melted a hole in the asphalt driveway.

The two entrances to Shoreview Drive were monitored by deputies who only allowed the vehicles of residents or Public Safety personnel to enter or leave. Still, hundreds of neighbors walked in and converged for a view of the damage. Gathering photo footage, three news station helicopters buzzed in and out like giant dragonflies.

Sheriff Chuck Hall looked into the still smoldering heap to see the ash and charred bone that was once a man where the driver's seat once was.

"Good riddance to that bastard." he thought to himself.

"Commissioner Largent was a good man." was the public statement the Sheriff spoke to the on scene reporter from the *County Sentinel*.

The police report would not be issued for a week, but Sheriff Hall knew what the obvious conclusion was: Commissioner Jerry Largent had awakened early. He had a single cup of coffee for breakfast. In the attempt to start his vehicle on Friday morning at 4:16 A.M., something exploded in his experimental car, either the high voltage lithium batteries in the trunk or the super combustible hydrogen fuel under the front hood. More than likely, both dangerous technologies reacted with each other in such a manner to completely annihilate all evidence that might reveal the specific cause of this tragic event. Commissioner Jerry Largent was killed and his body was literally cremated during the resulting incident.

By lunchtime, the national news stations were already reporting on this local accident. The universal spin was that electric and hydrogen powered cars were far too dangerous for experimentation by members of the public, especially elected officials who should know better.

Even Fox News, during the Mid-Day National News Round-Up, was editorializing that the Federal Government knows best when it comes to automotive technology.

Chapter 17 A Chance Encounter

Jerry's wet clothes hung from a nearby bush to dry out. He had pulled a fresh pair of jeans from his back pack. He was also grateful to have included the long sleeve flannel shirt in his provisions. The deer flies could not bite through either denim or thick cotton flannel which left few places of exposed skin for the insects to target in his new dry outfit. The wet work boots on his feet were a minor inconvenience as opposed to having no shoes at all.

All in all, Jerry Largent was in pretty good shape compared to the last guy who got into his car.

"Who was that in the flames? Did the hit man end up blowing himself up while he set the charges on the car? Will they assume that is my body or will an autopsy disclose the truth? How is Carla handling this?" More questions than answers rushed through his mind.

Jerry could not answer any of these questions but he could assess his present circumstances. He had forty-two dollars and some odd change from his wet clothes. The bills were drying out on a flat hot rock weighted by smaller rocks on top. All of his money would be consolidated into the change jar. That was also a good place to put his keys though the ones to the car would do him no good. The helicopters had flown away but he decided that darkness was his best cover. He calculated the incoming tide would be done by about nine P.M. that evening. He should make his way up the creek at the edge of dark to get maximum benefit of both tide and night.

He waited quietly under the tree attuned to the sounds of nature around him. A raucous kingfisher bird squawked in the distance along the creek but there was a rustling in the leaves that was moving closer to him.

A large two and a half foot long garter snake slithered down a short knoll above him and passed no more than three feet by Jerry who sat perfectly still against the trunk of the white oak. The harmless snake was no threat. Jerry simply admired the beautiful yellow, green, black and brown array of bright colors on this snake that must have recently molted.

The snake moved on in search of whatever snakes seek in the woods. Jerry put his head on his folded blanket and took a well-earned afternoon nap. He hoped the real snakes in the world had lost his trail.

The buzzing of mosquitoes in his face awoke Jerry from his dreamless sleep. The sun was going down. Jerry methodically collected his money from atop the rock and put it with his keys into the change jar. He folded his dry clothes from the bushes they hung upon. He put on a clean tee shirt and folded the flannel shirt.

The clothes and change jar were packed back in the back pack which was wrapped in the blanket that was dropped in the still watertight but muddy plastic bag. He strung his work boots together which again hung over his neck and shoulders.

As the sun was setting, Jerry Largent was outfitted in snorkeling gear back in the shallow depths of Indian Creek pushing his floating bag ahead of himself.

He had not gone far with the tide when he heard a snort from behind. He swiveled his head and shoulders as the sun faded into the Western horizon to be face to face with the ugliest, most monstrous creature he had ever seen.

His whole body convulsed in fear. The sound that emanated from the snorkel in his mouth can only be described as, "Bwaaahhh!!!"

Jerry Largent had smoothly survived death and incineration by not one, but two international hit men and all he could say was "Bwaaahhh!!!" when confronted with a true river monster.

The creature that looked something like a toothless walrus put its face under water and pushed past Jerry. It was every bit of ten feet long when the horizontal rounded tail slipped past him.

Jerry recognized the animal's distinctive posterior but could hardly believe what he was witnessing. He had seen these mammals from a distance in Florida but now he was swimming with a real live manatee in Maryland. The adrenalin from fear turned into joyful energy as Jerry swam with the gentle marine mammal up the creek in the moonlight. Together, they made their way up the main channel of the saltwater marsh.

They had traveled a few thousand yards when the channel ended in a flooded depression at the base of the freshwater stream from which the creek originated. The manatee stayed to drink in the freshwater while Jerry put on his boots and walked up the middle of the non-tidal narrow stream. He, too, was thirsty but was not prepared yet to drink water from the wild side of life.

He bid his new found friend good-bye and trudged up the shallow stream. The moon overhead cast a mirrored reflection on the surface guiding him through the woods. How far he had gone was beyond his estimation when he was overcome by a sense of familiarity.

Jerry moved from the stream bed. He worked his way up the bank and stumbled onto open ground. He recognized the cleared land in front of him under the light of the moon. This was the old swamp field on the farm his father once owned at the end of Mount Wolf Road.

He remembered working tobacco on this hot humid ground but the new owners had planted a fruit orchard in the fertile soil. Ripe apples, peaches, and pears hung from the short trees around him.

Jerry grabbed and bit into a soft, luscious peach. Nothing in this world ever tasted so good as that sweet fruit that at once satisfied his demanding thirst and the hunger that he had failed to recognize.

He ate another peach and decided to stick around in this little Garden of Eden for a bit.

In the moonlit orchard, Jerry Largent emptied his waterproof heavy duty trash bag. His wet clothes and snorkel gear went into that plastic bag. He put on dry jeans and the flannel shirt. He rolled the blanket and made a bedroll that he placed under the top flap of the back pack.

Jerry collected a small smorgasbord of apples, peaches, and pears that he put with the wet clothes and snorkel gear. He threw the plastic sack over his right shoulder. His back pack and blanket were strapped high on his back as he prepared to leave the swamp field paradise.

His work shoes were still saturated but, overall, his life was looking a whole lot better.

Chapter 18   The Big Send-off

Life was looking pretty good to the Friday night celebrants who were saturating themselves with liquor and beer at the bar and grill owned by St. Mary's County Government.

The Canoe Creek Golf Course closed at sundown but Commissioners Drake Alvey, James Lyons, and Kenny Leonard had called together the Democratic Central Committee, the Democratic Club, the St. Mary's County Youthful Order of Progressive Liberals and three members of the Ku Klux Klan for a special meeting to honor the memory of Commissioner Jerry Largent. Commissioner Doris Gunn-Manning had not been invited.   As a Republican, she was not welcome.   Not since Abraham Lincoln died in 1865, had so many Democrats in St. Mary's County gathered together to remember an elected official.   "Sheriff Hall are you sure our dear friend and fellow commissioner, Jerry Largent, has officially expired?" questioned Commissioner Drake Alvey after calling for a free round of drinks for everyone.

Sheriff Chuck Hall spun around, rose up from his bar stool, and stood before the joyful assembly. He said with his most professional voice, "The lone coffee cup in Commissioner Largent's sink was dusted for prints this afternoon.   Only his prints were found.   His wife who works at the Courthouse in LaPlata saw him in the flames. I, personally, saw the ashes and bits of burned bone that was once Jerry Largent. There is no evidence I can find of foul play.   I will waste no more tax dollars on the investigation and will release tomorrow his remains to be disposed of by his family. Bluntly speaking, Commissioner

Jerry Largent blew himself up experimenting with dangerous alternative energy technologies to power his vehicle and save money. He should have known better. Like they said on the Fox News Mid-Day Report, our Federal Government knows best what kind of cars we should drive."

A loud cheer from all attendees shook the walls of the bar and free drinks were handed to all. Silently, many questioned why their fellow Democratic Sheriff was watching Fox News at noon.

Then the toasts began:

"Here's to a future full of free lunch and BEER!" toasted Commissioner Kenny Leonard.

"Here's to a world free of accountability and transparency!" proclaimed Commissioner James Lyons.

"After a decade of watching our backsides, it's high time we get back to business as usual. And, another round of free drinks for all!" Commissioner Drake Alvey clinched the three-way round as the celebrants cheered and raised their glasses in support. By dying, Commissioner Jerry Largent had become a very popular guy with this Democratic congregation.

While his Democratic friends were toasting his untimely demise, Commissioner Jerry Largent was walking down the gravel road through the farm his father once owned. He was upset when his Dad sold it but that day was done. This night, he was happy to have eaten a couple peaches.

Upon reaching Mount Wolf Road, Jerry Largent opted to hike close to the woods should a car pass by. He did not wish to be seen or recognized. Probably, his picture had been posted throughout the instant media of television or Internet. As a local elected official, he was somewhat well known. A politician blown up in a car would be far more publicly recognizable, at least from the photos taken prior to the explosion.

The two mile trip was slow going. When he heard a vehicle coming or saw the lights of a car far in the distance, he simply eased into the nearby bushes covering his face behind the dark trash bag. He was fortunate to not be allergic to poison ivy because he surely was making numerous contacts with the dreaded native weed.

He lost track of how many cars had passed and how many times he had melted into the underbrush along the County road before he arrived in the Town Center of Charlotte Hall about twenty-four hours after his car had burst into flames.

Charlotte Hall Town Center is a primarily commercial strip of highway along Three Notch Road north of where the History and High-Tech Highways merge. There is minimum residential development and no sidewalks connecting the retail sites. The dark open space behind the box stores gave Jerry quicker travel time to work his way to the destination he had planned deep in the woods beside Indian Creek.

He stopped at the newspaper boxes beside the public commuter parking lot. No one was around. The busses to DC do not run on the weekend. Of course, the Friday issue of the bi-weekly *County Sentinel* did not carry news of his death. They had gone to print on Thursday afternoon while he was still alive. The national papers did not have anything on the front page.

A new bright yellow news box at the end of the row caught his attention.

"Commissioner Jerry Largent Killed in Fiery Inferno" was the headline on the front page of the *Seventh Sun*. The tabloid had just hit the street in the vending machine delivered by Bardog Nelson from his pick-up truck a few minutes before Jerry arrived.

Jerry smiled as he admired the picture of himself and his car in the parking lot of the White Neck Bar and Grill. The flames superimposed on either side made for a thrilling front page.

"Foul Play Suspected" was the caption below. Jerry dug beneath the blanket on top of his clothes for the change jar in his back pack. He unscrewed the lid, put his keys in his pants pocket, and dug out four quarters before screwing the top on and putting the jar back in his pack.

He had no problem putting four of his precious quarters into the machine. He was happy to spend a buck on the first edition of Punkin Nelson's new newspaper. He carefully folded it under his left arm.

Behind the next shopping center, Jerry passed by an exposed outdoor faucet between the buildings. He turned the handle and drank from the stream of highly chlorinated water. He washed his face and hands and moved on.

Daylight was just beginning to creep into the sky. Jerry eased into a display lot full of mini-barns that were placed in front of his lumber yard.

Prior to becoming a County Commissioner, entrepreneur Jerry Largent had allowed a local Mennonite mini-barn builder from sleepy Bishop Road to display an assortment of his brightly colored barns along this section of commercial roadway.

In one mini-barn, Jerry put an electric scooter and bike shop for him to use on the weekends to market affordable, environmentally sensible transportation.

Most of his potential customers sought gasoline powered go-karts or mini-bikes for their kids. The few electric scooters he sold mostly went to high octane drag racers who wanted low maintenance pit bikes at the track. He closed the no profit shop and ran for public office.

There was no time to question human logic or conditioning as he pulled his keys out of his pocket and unlocked the sealed mini-barn at the back of the lot. Jerry Largent slipped inside, closed the door, and fumbled in the darkness to find an open space to lie down and rest.

Chapter 19 Home Sweet Home

The tick crawling on his neck roused Jerry Largent from sleep on the hard plywood floor. He pinched the hard little bug between his fingers and looked around the dimly lit shed.

He spotted a medium size crowbar.

That was overkill for a tick but just the tool to slip through the inside door handle to effectively lock the shed from outside intrusion. With the crowbar in place, Jerry crushed the tick between the head of a large bolt and the nut that he unscrewed from it.

Jerry stripped completely and carefully checked from his feet first to the top of his head for any ticks that might have imbedded themselves in his body during his journey through woods and bushes of Southern Maryland. He was not terribly concerned with the common dog ticks like the one he just smashed the life out of.

Of greater concern to him were the soft tiny deer ticks that transmit Lyme Disease. Jerry could not afford to get sick. Dead people can't go to doctors.

Jerry Largent was especially conscious to check the seam around the top of his head where his hairpiece met his existing hair. Jerry's one submission to ego was his monthly trip to Men's Hair Unlimited. He parted with a hundred bucks every month to have what little was left of his real hair, cut and colored. The hairpiece was also color matched and re-glued to his head.

Though he was approaching his sixty year mark, Jerry easily passed as a man hardly forty. There was not a hint of grey or baldness to be seen in his well styled hair thanks to Men's Hair Unlimited in Alexandria, Virginia.

Assured that he was as tick free as possible, in this shed full of tools and metal parts, Jerry tried to get his bearings.

He had no idea what time it was. There was a gentle rain falling outside which was keeping the temperature reasonably comfortable within the mini-barn. Light filtered through plastic opaque campaign signs that Jerry had long ago used drywall screws to secure across the inside window frames. This effectively kept out the prying eyes of potential thieves. Though no one could see in from outside, Jerry put on a pair of shorts from his back pack and took notice of the stuff that surrounded him.

While Commissioner Jerry Largent was surveying his new headquarters, Carla Largent had returned from the hospital and looked through the living room window and the rain at the burned hulk of the car now rusting in her driveway. She watched a Sheriff's Deputy patrol car pull up. The Deputy opened the trunk and pulled out a large half full trash bag. She greeted him at the door. He explained the contents of the bag, put it on the porch, and left.

"My husband deserves a more fitting coffin than a trash bag." thought Carla but she had no better idea at the moment. She returned to her private grief in the quiet house. The bag of Fast Freddy's ashes remained on the porch in Golden Beach.

Three decades of alternative energy projects surrounded a very live Jerry Largent in his poorly lit headquarters less than a stone's throw from busy dual lane Three Notch Road. The pear he was having for breakfast, lunch, or dinner was moist, sweet, and delicious. He chose an apple for dessert.

In a cedar cabinet, there were old vapor carburetors that he experimented with during his years as a mate and boat captain in Key Largo. Parts of electric scooters cluttered the floor and an unsold senior style electric tricycle took up a lot of space. On one of the shelves was a whole array of hydrogen generators that Jerry had built before he finally came to understand for the need of an additional circuit in the electrolytic process. There was even a seized up nine horsepower diesel motor that he had run on homemade bio-diesel fuel. Too bad he forgot to put oil in the crankcase of the new engine.

Jerry Largent never claimed to be perfect.

Quietly, he organized the treasure trove of junk around him. Being Saturday, it was likely someone might stop by the display lot to pick up a directional flyer from the main display shed but the crowbar jammed through the inside door handle insured that no one could easily enter this mini-barn. There was no salesman ever on the lot. The portable barns were only there for display, a hook on the highway to direct the potential buyer to Hiram Stauffer's shop on Bishop Road.

Satisfied that he was prepped for another day, Jerry unfolded his *Seventh Sun* newspaper. Directly under the limited light passing through his old political sign that pledged "Affordable Sober Leadership" Commissioner Jerry Largent read about the gory details of his horrible death as reported by Punkin Nelson.

Punkin also documented her earlier meeting with Commissioner Largent two days before he died when she snapped his picture with her camera phone. She described the importance of the technology Jerry Largent used to power his car to both improve our national economy and clean up the environment for everyone in the world. She also disclosed Commissioner Largent's out-of-character consumption of a cold beer. Something fishy had taken place and the *Seventh Sun* was going to get the scoop.

"Good for you Punkin." Jerry thought as he finished the weekly tabloid and wondered how the *County Sentinel* would spin the same events when it hit the street on Tuesday.

Chapter 20 Politics as Usual

The first issue of the *Seventh Sun* newspaper had completely sold out by the time darkness enveloped Jerry Largent in his mini-barn refuge in the middle of the busy Charlotte Hall Town Center.

Punkin Nelson was already working on a big story from the night before.

Carla Largent had gone to bed early, exhausted from grief. A Mona Lisa smile was on her lips as she dreamed of playing with her eternally young daughter. Oddly enough, Jerry Largent had not joined them.

Jerry Largent was dressed in fresh jeans and tee shirt. His filet knife and sheath hung from his belt. His ear was pressed against the door of the dark shed. He was listening to traffic passing in front. Between the two traffic lights north that controlled Golden Beach traffic and south where Route 6 crossed Three Notch Road was a flat spot where there was virtually no traffic in either direction for a few seconds. He did not have a watch. He sensed the rhythm. When he felt the time was right, Jerry smoothly lifted the crowbar from the handle and eased out the door. He quickly closed and locked the door behind him with his key as he slid into the shadows between the mini-barns on the lot.

In the cool shadows and freedom of the open night, Jerry Largent assessed his situation. The rain had stopped but the remaining clouds in the sky obscured much of the moonlight. He could go pretty much where he wanted as long as he stayed out of sight. And, the work boots on his feet were almost dry.

His confidence grew as he moved away from the lights of town back into his old mill building at the rear side of the property. No one was welcome here and there was a local rumor that bad things happened to bad people who trespassed on the Largent Lumberyard.

"A bad reputation can be a good thing." thought Jerry Largent as he walked down the broken asphalt road that he had traveled by forklift on a daily basis for a quarter century. He smiled at the political irony.

Though the big mill had been dismantled, there were many empty five gallon buckets that once held motor or hydraulic oil in the old mill building. Of the yellow, white, black or blue colors, Jerry wisely chose a black bucket to carry his evening provisions.

He pulled a converted 55 gallon trash barrel from beneath the big pole shed to better see inside. Prior to scrounging in the depths of the receptacle, he shook it and stepped back. No sense getting bit by a coon or possum or being sprayed by a skunk.

Assured the container was uninhabited, Jerry sifted through the many soda cans, 7-11 coffee cups, and plastic soda bottles, to pull out a couple 32 ounce Gatorade bottles that he had himself thrown in just last week.

He lifted the handle on the outdoor spigot pipe beside the mill building and let the water flow a few seconds before drinking long and hard from the stream of water that came from a fifty year old shallow well. Unlike the treated water from the public water system Jerry had drunk early that morning, this water was cool and naturally sweet. He rinsed the two Gatorade bottles, filled them with water, and put them in his bucket. Then, with the bucket in his left hand and a lumber stacking stick cane in his right, Jerry moved to the next aisle of his Saturday night shopping spree.

Other residents of St. Mary's County were also drinking heavily that evening. In the bar and grill of the Canoe Creek County Golf Course, Commissioner Drake Alvey called for another round of free drinks for the members of the Democratic organizations who had come together again to toast, roast, and eulogize their dear friend from across the aisle, Republican Commissioner Jerry Largent.

Sheriff Chuck Hall was notably absent but no one noted his absence.

Instead, with their tongues loosened by too many rounds of free beer and liquor, Commissioners Alvey, Lyons, and Leonard bragged about the many times they had organized to snooker Commissioner Largent. At first, the politically partisan celebrants laughed in unison at the stories that involved prioritizing outvoting a fellow commissioner over sensible public policy.

The laughter grew quieter with each story as the realization saturated each attendee individually that the very real problems plaguing their County: high taxes, excessive drug use, rampant crime, and overdevelopment, had been inflicted upon them by the three commissioners who were denigrating Commissioner Jerry Largent.

"And, we dumped six million dollars into a piece of swampland rather than accept the high ground that Largent was able to get donated!" Commissioner James Lyons said as he finished another story and slapped the backs of the two commissioners on either side of him. All three laughed loudly.

But, by this time, no one else did. Commissioner Drake Alvey was first to respond to the deafening silence. "Another round of free drinks!" he declared.

Commissioner Kenny Leonard echoed, "Yes, more free beer!"

The crowd may have been inebriated but they were not stupid. One by one, the celebrants put down their glasses and solemnly walked out the door.

In just a few minutes, there were only four people left sitting around a single table in the Canoe Neck Golf Course bar and grill. Commissioners Alvey, Lyons, and Leonard sat with Buster Butler and stared at the empty glasses in front of them. Even the bartender had gone home.

The conversation was more animated between the six members of the Republican Central Committee in the backroom of the Pax River Lounge in Lexington Park.

None of the four men and two women who were elected to this office had been born in St. Mary's County. There were three members who supported Commissioner Largent's homespun common sense philosophy while the other three members favored aligning with the wealthy Democratic developers as part of a free market agenda. The lone swing vote of this seven member board had resigned six months ago due to the pressures that had been foisted upon her.

The two women sat on opposite sides of the divided central committee. Margaret Miller was a common sense conservative while Kathleen Knutson held the wealthy elite position. The men quietly subjugated themselves to these forceful women who dominated the debate.

That Saturday evening, the debate focused on whether the Republicans should move ahead advertising for a new central committee member or should they wait till the North End Commissioner position was officially open and jointly advertise, thus saving money.

Both sides wanted another committee member in support of their agenda but neither side wanted the other side to get a member to have the majority of votes. They had not even considered their choices for County Commissioner in just a day's time.

Then, there was the issue of the first issue of this new County newspaper.

"The *Seventh Sun* might be a cheaper place to advertise these positions." Margie stated.

"The *County Sentinel* has more stability and readership, so it is a better deal at twice the price." countered Kathleen.

Ultimately, the Republican Central Committee deadlocked after two hours of pointless discussion.

They left the lounge on Saturday night at 10:00 P.M. with the unanimous consensus that they would do nothing.

Chapter 21
Basic Food and Transportation

Jerry Largent knew for a while that he must remain in the dark at the edge of civilization. His thirst had been well quenched. His shoes were dry enough. The fruit he had eaten over the past two days was healthy and delicious. He was in pretty darned good shape for a dead man.

He knew he had been targeted by an international hit man. He had befriended and swam with a renegade manatee. And, to his knowledge, he had completely avoided all human contact. All this had happened over the last couple days.

There was only one thing officially deceased Commissioner Jerry Largent wished for in life as he slipped through the shadows at the far edge of Charlotte Hall.

Jerry Largent wanted a cheeseburger.

He had more than enough money to buy a cheeseburger but he could not show his face anywhere.

The McDonalds in Charlotte Hall stayed open 24 hours a day, 7 days a week, busy during the day and well lit at night. The nearby Burger King was closed and the staff had gone home. Jerry could raid the BK dumpster for a leftover cheeseburger discarded in the evening trash.

He was not too proud to pull something from the trash to eat but the possible presence of security cameras around the franchise kept him at bay. He was far too recognizable to blow his cover over a cheeseburger.

He wandered through the shadows of the open stalls in the nearby flea market. There were no security cameras here as most of the weekend based businesses were transient. At the lone farm produce dealer's stand, he looked through empty fruit and vegetable boxes to find a cornucopia of vegetarian delight.

Tomatoes with soft spots were buried in the pile. Cantaloupes and watermelons that had either split in the sun or been cut to sample had been cast aside too. Jerry picked a few of the best melons and tomatoes and put them in the bottom of his bucket.

When he slipped back into his Mennonite constructed hideaway well before daylight, Jerry Largent had plenty of food and drink to get him through a day of rest on Sunday.

But, he still wanted a cheeseburger.

Carla Largent only wanted to sleep forever. She finally got up late on Sunday morning with the sun burning through her bedroom window. She started the coffee pot and looked at the trash that Jerry had not taken out.

She sealed the plastic garbage bag with a twist tie and carried it into the garage. She picked up the other bag of trash from the week before, opened the garage door, and carried both bags past the burned car to the street for Monday morning pick-up.

This was the first of many new duties that she would inherit.

She sat with her coffee at the kitchen table looking over the mouth of Indian Creek. Normally, when someone dies, the funeral home takes care of the details for burial or cremation as well as public notification.

The fire had taken care of the first task and the media was covering the notification process. Carla decided to release the ashes of her husband far out into the blue waters of the Gulf Stream that flow past the Florida Keys. She missed those cool evenings with Jerry on the night fishing party boat trips so many years ago. She regretted not going on that last catfish catching trip he took up Indian Creek on Monday afternoon.

She also remembered her last real conversation with Jerry about the Diego Garcia co-incidence they witnessed together during the week. It gave Carla a sense of solace to know that, in spite of every tragedy, God has a purpose and plan. Indeed, She does have a sense of humor.

Carla smiled and resolved to find a church to join in the days ahead.

The Sunday afternoon sun heated up the locked mini-barn in front of the Largent Lumberyard. Dressed only in his one pair of under shorts, Jerry was perspiring in the warm still air within his refuge of solitude. He had eaten a full brunch of watermelon, cantaloupe, and tomato filets that he had trimmed the bad portions from with his sharp knife. The fruit and vegetable waste lay in the bottom of his bucket to be tossed into the bushes during his next evening venture.

He was lucky it was not hotter in the shed where it was either twilight or pitch dark depending on day or night. July had been a month of record heat and August was now cooler than normal. The temperature in the mini-barn was only in the low-ninety degree range. Any other August, it would have been a real sweat box.

Jerry was counting his blessings as he calculated his next moves.

"I must become unrecognizable." Jerry thought and realized how nature would do that for him.

"Also, I need transportation." He would have to do that for himself.

He discounted assembling one of the quick little electric scooters that lay in parts around him.

"A man riding a kids' scooter might attract unnecessary attention." reasoned Jerry Largent. "However, an old timer casually pedaling on a senior tricycle should go pretty much unnoticed." He turned his attention to the pedal assisted electric trike on the floor in front of him.

After inflating the tires with a hand pump in the former shop, Jerry turned his attention to getting the trike to run. He put a battery tester from his tool assortment on the four small sealed lead acid batteries that were standard issue with the bike. They were all stone cold dead. Jerry knew they were not rechargeable. He should not waste his time trying.

He needed a bigger battery pack with longer range.

Under the work shelf, there was a stack of Blue Top Optima batteries that had come from his MR2 when he converted to the lithium pack. Jerry chose the two that tested best. He correctly wired them into the 24 volt series circuit that fed the electric motor. The two large batteries fit almost perfectly into the frames where the four dead batteries were once housed but the Blue Tops extended nearly twice as high above the two racks.

Jerry estimated that this arrangement would give him about fifty miles of range at a sedate speed of ten miles per hour.

He set the rear axle frame up and across a concrete block so both wheels cleared the floor. He flipped the on switch and the on/off indicator light lit up. Gingerly, Jerry pushed the accelerator control switch of the ElecTrike brand three wheeler with his thumb. Both wheels spun freely.

Elated, he shut off the power switch to focus on how to charge up the batteries.

The mini-barn Jerry was sweating within was the only one on the lot locked from the inside. It was also the only shed of the display that had two solar panels secured outside to the roof.

Rather than connect to the grid, he used these two 75 watt solar panels to charge scooter batteries when he ran the electric bike and scooter business ten years ago. When Jerry closed the shop, he bugged off the wires which he left in place. They would be easy to reconnect.

In less than an hour, the deep cycle batteries in the senior tricycle were absorbing free solar power from the hot sun beating down on the roof of the secured shed. Jerry had even wired in a voltage regulator to keep the batteries from overcharging.

Jerry Largent had accomplished a lot of work when he slipped out of the portable barn that Sunday evening to forage for food and supplies.

His work boots were dry. But, he still wanted a cheeseburger.

Chapter 22 From Under the Rug

Jeremy Buckner was riding the rear bumper garbage pick-up position on the County compactor trash truck as the sun was rising out of the Calvert County horizon across the Patuxent River from the Largent home at the mouth of Indian Creek. Golden Beach was scheduled on Monday mornings for the public garbage collection service run by St. Mary's County Government.

Jeremy was not the sharpest tack in the box but he was a dependable County employee who appreciated his job keeping his County clean. When he missed the County Transit bus to work one morning, Commissioner Largent gave him a ride to County Government in the little electric sports car that was now crispy fried and wrapped in yellow plastic barrier tape in the driveway on Shoreview Drive.

He threw the two bags near the street into the compactor bin and spotted the other garbage bag tied up on the front porch of the Largent residence. Jeremy jogged over to the porch, grabbed the bag, and threw it in with the rest of the garbage.

He had liked Commissioner Largent and would do what he could to help his widow.

Assistant Fire Marshall Stephen Waterford had arrived early to his office on the other side of the Patuxent River in Prince Frederick, the County Seat of Calvert County. The fire in Commissioner Largent's vehicle was a hotter, more complete burn than anything he had witnessed. By the time his supervisor arrived, he had a dozen ash samples labeled for specific chemical tests to target possible combustive accelerants.

"The Largent Case is closed. No chemical analysis will be needed." Fire Marshall Sajid Ravishnu informed his assistant.

"But, Sir," Waterford countered, "This was a highly publicized fire with the loss of an elected official. Should we not make an official investigation?"

"An elected official who should have known better than experiment with lethal technology! Hydrogen gas and lithium batteries are a dangerous combination. Everyone knows that. The St. Mary's County Sheriff has closed the case and we will do so as well. Case closed!" ordered Fire Marshall Ravishnu.

While a very confused Stephen Waterford returned the samples to the storage room, Sajid Ravishnu wondered how best he might spend the ten thousand dollar cash incentive he had received over the weekend to let the Largent investigation slide.

Arthur Ching was parked in a campground on the Conestoga River in Pennsylvania working on his computer. Arthur, or Jung Fang as he preferred to be named, was collecting information on a politically up and coming State legislator who would be found dead from a drug overdose before the end of the week.

Sheriff Chuck Hall was not in his office. He had taken a two week leave of absence. Captain Robert Langley was in charge of the St. Mary's County Sheriff's Department during the interim.

Jerry Largent was stripped back down to his under shorts, locked in his personal prison on the sales lot. The traditional August heat had returned after a relatively cool weekend. He would have to stay still and sweat out the day. The perspiration from his head was mixing with the glue under his hair piece to loosen the coifed arrangement.

He was due for his monthly trip to Hair Unlimited but that day was done. Dead men don't get their wigs adjusted.

Largent decided to accept his baldness. After all, he had come to accept his own death.

He shook his head as he realized the hard truth, "Some elected officials come out of the closet. Too bad I had to die to come out from under the rug."

Jerry found an old bottle of orange scented hand cleaner in the shed. He needed a solvent to separate the remaining glue still bound to the skin on his scalp. He gradually worked the pleasant smelling lotion under the wig and slowly separated the hair piece from his skin. The hairdressers at Hair Unlimited had specific products to accomplish this process. However, the hand cleaner worked pretty well.

When he was done, he tossed the fake clump of hair into the black plastic bucket with the fruit and vegetable scraps from the meal he just consumed. He worked more of the orange smelling hand cleaner over his bald head to dissolve the remaining glue and wiped off the top of his head with one of the towels he had stuffed in his back pack.

If he had a mirror, Jerry Largent would have checked himself out. He knew he was not pretty. He probably looked like Bozo, the Clown. But, he was a lot more comfortable.

Carla Largent had slept far past morning. The Southern Maryland humidity and heat of the afternoon sun was a stark contrast to the cool air conditioned home she left to check her mail box on the street.

She grabbed a stack of junk mail and a few letters. She noticed the two bags of trash had been picked up. Responding to afterthought, Carla looked up to the front porch.

The bag containing her husband's ashes was gone!

She clutched the mail to her chest and ran to both sides of the porch. The bag had not blown over. She ran around the house in a desperate search for the partially filled heavy duty plastic bag.

With tears in her eyes, she entered her cool home. She was completely demoralized from the events that had occurred. She had no friends. There was no one she could call. Jerry Largent was her husband, only friend, best fishing buddy. Now, he was gone. There were not even ashes to cast into the wind.

"Carlos is the only family I have left." Carla thought but she had not heard from him in thirty years. She did not know how to contact him.

She pulled the mail from in front of her breasts and sorted through. A priority envelope with a simple post office box return address piqued her curiosity. The handwriting on the letter addressed to her was beyond familiar.

Carla's hands shook with anticipation as she opened the envelope. A check made out to Carla Largent for a thousand dollars from Colu-Miami Condo Rentals LLC was inside with a handwritten note:

"This is your monthly rent payment from the condo we own in South Miami. I will collect and send the rent to you each month. Your Brother, Carlos."

"Diego Garcia!" Carla exclaimed. Only she would know why.

The Board of Elections Office in the Governmental Center outside of Leonardtown was almost ready to close that Monday afternoon when Buster Butler walked in at 4:23 P.M. to pick up a change of registration form. He filled it out and returned it to the supervisor who recorded the information in her computer and placed the paper form in the files. Buster Butler was now officially a Republican.

Chapter 23 Return of the Ring

"Thank you, Carlos," was the simple salutation headlining the letter that Carla Largent embarked upon that evening. In her native Spanish language, she related the three decades of her good life with Jerry.

She scripted page after page of personal memories for her brother to read. She held nothing back as tears of sadness and relief flowed from her soft brown eyes. The letter was a combination of funeral and eulogy for Jerry with the private diary of the triumphs and tragedies of two lovers from two very different parts of the world. She concluded her letter simply as Carlos had done, "Your Sister, Carla".

Long after midnight, Carla Largent addressed a big manila envelope to C. Castaneda with the Miami address. She inserted the many page letter with some news clippings of her husband's political successes and a couple of the recent death reports. She also included a very precious palm card memorializing little Carlena from her funeral. In the morning, she would drive to the post office and purchase enough stamps to send the heavy envelope. She resolved to go back to work on Wednesday.

Jerry Largent was also at work in the central boiler room of the three dry kilns on the lumberyard. In the hot humid darkness, he was shaving the rest of his head using the disposable razor and bar of soap he had tossed into his back pack prior to his death. He lathered out of another bucket of hot water he had drawn from the reservoir that pre-fed the boiler. Jerry threw clumps of his own severed hair into the black bucket with the wig and food scraps.

It took time and patience. Jerry had plenty of both. After he felt carefully with the tips of his fingers to assure he cut off all the hair above his ears and behind his head, he rubbed his stubbly beard. Jerry had not shaved since the admonition by Carlos one week ago. He had been too preoccupied.

"The beard can grow." He thought. "It might make a good cover."

Jerry unscrewed the bolts around the cleanout door of the boiler's firebox. He swung the heavy metal door open and threw the contents of his black bucket into the bed of burning sawdust. He closed and sealed the door. In a short while, his wig, hair, and food scraps had been incinerated.

He rinsed his night camouflage bucket with the warm soapy water he had used to shave with. Jerry tossed the dirty water into the poison ivy vines that crept up a nearby shed. Jerry Largent returned for a late night nap in his mini-barn.

Most of St. Mary's County was in deep sleep when, Jerry arose from the blanket he lay on before dawn and headed for the depths of the woods behind the mill property. He was not about to spend another day cooking in a hot storage shed.

Commissioner Jerry Largent was noted as absent at the St. Mary's County Commissioners meeting that morning. He was remembered in the opening prayer. The remaining four commissioners approved the weekly bills with no discussion. Three of the commissioners could barely contain themselves as the vote was taken. On page 97, the combined liquor and beer bill for the weekend celebration at the Canoe Neck County Golf Course bar and grill totaled $9,426.84. With a swift unanimous vote, the expenditure slipped thru in the large stack.

Commissioner Doris Gunn-Manning had better things to do than review bills.

Carla Largent was weighing her manila envelope in the Charlotte Hall Post Office while her husband was less than a half mile away in a cool stream ravine weighing his options.

Kilpeck Creek is the main feeder stream for Trent Hall Creek which is the next run down the Patuxent River from Indian Creek. Jerry Largent had spent much of his youth tromping through the swamp behind his home place at the head of the stream. His entry into the world of politics was precipitated by his involvement in a community water quality issue over industrial development downstream.

No one else wanted to get involved in the political process so Jerry put his name on the ballot. The rest is a matter of local history.

Now, his life had come full circle as he tried to see his reflection in a quiet ripple free pool.

His pasty white bald head shone brightly in the water like a full moon rising overhead. The beard was harder to see as it had not grown out fully. Looking closely, he saw mostly grey whiskers on the reflection looking back at him from the pool. A small crayfish crept across the clay bottom.

Jerry Largent did not recognize his own reflection except for one feature. The piercing steel grey eyes that stared back at him were undeniably his.

A college girlfriend had once called his eyes "squinty". Obviously, she did not become his wife. Jerry Largent's most distinctive characteristic was his piercing steel blue eyes that looked deep into the soul of a person and the heart of the matter. In reality, Jerry Largent was slightly nearsighted but he refused to wear glasses. He squeezed his eyelids tight to bring the world into better focus.

A Whirl-a-gig swimming beetle swam across his reflection. Whirl-a-gig beetles are also called Kissing Bugs. Legend says that you can kiss a Kissing Bug and it will spell out the name of the person you will marry when it is placed back on the water. Jerry Largent knew better. He had tried that hypothesis many years ago in a creek that flowed through a meadow behind his grandmother's farm in nearby Mechanicsville.

Jerry Largent spotted a small round object protruding from the bottom not far from where the crawdad made its path. He eased knee deep into the water and pulled up a grey ring from the depths of the pool.

A flood of buried memories swelled through his brain as he polished the tarnished solid silver class ring on his tee shirt. This heavy ring with no stone came from Leonard Hall Junior Naval Academy which is located at the Leonardtown Governmental Center Campus. Jerry was sure this was the same ring he had lost many years ago.

He remembered the circumstances:

Jerry was assembling a high school science project on "The Auditory Organs of Fish". Armed with a fine mesh dip net and permission from Mrs. Alice Somerville whose husband owned the property, Jerry was dip netting the creek for Blacknose Dace, a common stream minnow.

He must have dropped the cherished ring out of his shirt top pocket when he bent over to push the net under the bank where he caught his best specimens.

The lost ring that symbolized surviving four years of strict middle school military education under the tutelage of Catholic Xaverian Brothers was never replaced, not by a high school, college, or wedding ring. For some unexplained reason, Jerry Largent refused to wear a ring again.

He placed the tarnished ring on his right little finger. His ring fingers had grown too large.

Jerry Largent moved up to a mossy natural grotto above the stream. He sat cross legged on the soft ground, put his hands on his knees, and closed his eyes.

He drifted into a deep state of meditative realization. The ring on his finger would become his constant reminder that he was, is, and will never be alone.

His old class ring had become his most valued commodity.

But, he still wanted a cheeseburger.

Chapter 24 A Sobering Experience

Either by land or by sea, the trip to their secret meeting in Colonial Beach was not nearly as festive as the previous week for the four St. Mary's County Commissioners who planned to meet with Captain Robert Langley. He was expected to deliver an update on the status of Sheriff Chuck Hall.

Commissioner Kenny Leonard was tasked with keeping Commissioner Doris Gunn-Manning clueless regarding the celebration that had occurred over the weekend at the Canoe Creek County Golf Course bar and grill. While they traveled to the Lucky Strike Casino in his new Town Car, Commissioner Leonard focused the conversation on the loss of Commissioner Largent.

"Tough deal for Largent, huh?" Kenny grunted.

"Yeah, but we've got to move on. I heard that Buster Butler lives in that District and he is a registered Republican. It sure would be good to have a real businessman on our Board." said Doris.

"Busta Butt's a Republican? Will wonders never cease?" said Kenny.

While Commissioners Leonard and Gunn-Manning were discussing Buster Butler's political status and Commissioners Alvey and Lyons were making their way across the Potomac River by County yacht, Jerry Largent was trespassing on Buster's property.

He was following the stream on the old Somerville Farm back to the grist mill pond he remembered so well. When the winter warmed at the end of February or early March every year, Jerry would take some time to witness the toads mating and laying their eggs. When Buster Butler bought the farm, Jerry stopped his simple rite of spring.

His permission slip came from Mrs. Somerville, not Buster Butler.

Upon reaching the little pond, Jerry was shocked to find the wetland had disappeared. The habitat had been filled with gravel and graded over. Busta Butt was up to something but it had nothing to do with securing environmental permits. And, Jerry had no permission to be there.

Jerry called the situation a draw for the time being and sauntered back through his old sawmill operation as the sun was going down. He stopped in a tool shed and picked up an old pair of wrap-around dark glasses that he used when cutting metal with an acetylene torch in his past life.

His distinctive eyes were not to be seen behind the cool shades. He was now virtually unrecognizable from the Commissioner Jerry Largent who graced the cover of the *Seventh Sun* weekly newspaper that weekend.

In the dark commuter parking lot in Charlotte Hall, Jerry passed by the newspaper machine that held the latest copy of the *County Sentinel*. Already, he was old news as a terrible accident in the Seventh District involving a Sheriff's Department car and a promising student/athlete was headlined on the front page:

"Student Killed by On-Duty Sheriff's Car, Alcohol Use Suspected"

Jerry had seen many such horrific headlines in St. Mary's County. He decided to save his quarters for some peanut butter and cheese crackers at a nearby vending machine before slipping back into his no-tell motel room on the mini-barn lot.

He could catch the real story in the *Seventh Sun* on Saturday morning.

It was time for Jerry to catch a little shuteye. He had to wake before daybreak.

Commissioners Kenny Leonard and Doris Gunn-Manning were somberly driving home from Colonial Beach following the revelations delivered by Captain Robert Langley of the St. Mary's Sheriff's Department.

Commissioner Leonard did not know what to say and Commissioner Gunn-Manning did not know what to think. The result was silence.

Commissioners Drake Alvey and James Lyons were stunned into temporary temperance as they cruised home on the County yacht "Bottoms Up". Ginny Lyons did not have to worry about her man driving home drunk as she waited in the parking lot of the Canoe Creek Marina. Duck and Jimbo were stone cold sober. The cooler on board full of ten ounce Budweiser beer cans had been barely touched.

Jerry Largent was not in the dark as he took inventory for his next cruising adventure.

After closing and barring the door of his mini-barn, Jerry reached across the handlebars to flip on the headlight switch of his ElecTrike senior tricycle. The two fully charged deep cycle Optima batteries had over a thousand watts of free energy to expend that Jerry had tapped from the two solar panels on the roof.

He used just a few watts to light up the shed and assemble needed provisions.

The rod and reel combo and little tackle box went into his back pack first. In went his filet knife and sheath. A knife and sheath hanging from his belt was an invitation to legal hassles. His gun would stay in the shed. He tossed in a 24 volt scooter charger that plugged into a standard AC receptacle. Jerry Largent was always looking ahead.

His head, however, was a little on the sore side. Though he had spent most of his day in the woods, there had been enough sun creeping through the canopy to put a slight burn on Jerry's freshly bald head. He could not stand a whole day in the sun without appropriate cover.

Jerry rummaged through his shed for a ball cap. When he opened the bottom doors of the cedar cabinet, he was greeted by an old guitar case that he had long forgotten. Inside the case was an Epiphone acoustic guitar that he had kept in the shop for personal entertainment while he waited for a possible scooter customer. Though the American made instrument from Kalamazoo had seen a decade of temperature changes, the neck was straight. The strings were not too rusty. Jerry had met his traveling companion.

He gently placed the guitar back in its case and continued his search for the right headgear.

On a nail driven into a 2x4 support stud, a doo-rag hung inconspicuously. Jerry spotted the red, white, and blue biker's bandana that was given to him as a joke by Carla when he opened the electric scooter shop. It would come in handy now.

Jerry turned off the headlight switch, laid down his tender head on a folded towel and closed his eyes. He wishfully rubbed the solid silver ring on the little finger of his right hand. In the morning, he would be ready to roll.

Chapter 25 On the Road Again

The Detroit 1292 diesel engine in the St. Mary's County Commissioners' yacht was cooling down from the weekly Colonial Beach trip as the "Bottoms Up" bobbed secure in her slip at the Canoe Neck Marina.

Most people in Southern Maryland were sound asleep while Jerry Largent prepared for his first day in the public since his "death" five days ago.

He eased his modified ElecTrike senior tricycle out of the mini-barn. With a back pack full of fishing gear, basic provisions and his last apple, Jerry eased into the night powered by a quiet electric motor fueled by photons provided by the sun.

He cruised through the early morning darkness free of many of the addictions that had been part of his life less than a week ago. Jerry had not had a cup of coffee since that last cup when his car blew up. He had not blogged on the Internet in his favorite energy discussion forums. Jerry had not even turned on a computer. He had not seen any television or listened to a radio. He did not even have a phone!

If he was wearing a straw hat and driving a horse and buggy, Jerry Largent with his stubbly grizzled grey beard might have passed for an Amish man. However, he was sporting a red, white, and blue bandana on his head and pedaling a motorized three wheeler on the County maintained hiker biker trail as the sun came up. Jerry could have easily been a resident from the veterans' home or a patriotic senior cruising from a housing development nearby.

As Carla Largent was commuting to her job on Route 6, Jerry Largent had just passed the intersection where Route 6 and the bike trail intersect near the North County Library. Carla did not see him and he did not recognize her car.

She was intent on getting to work and he was focused on the woman walking her dog on the trail. She was his first human contact since his self-imposed exile. What might her reaction be?

Jerry tried to avert his gaze behind his dark wrap-around sunglasses as he checked for any reaction from the woman. Only her dog yipped a bit. She took no notice of the old codger on the trike. He was no threat, no one but an old man pedaling on a three wheeler.

Emboldened, Jerry cruised up and down the trail passing hikers and bikers even smiling and waving as he passed. He was a person once again. Not the same person, but a member of the human race, nonetheless.

Rather than push his luck further, Jerry took a gravel road from the trail that headed to a pond deep in the woods. He dug some worms and grubs from under a rotted log and flipped a baited hook, split shot and bobber rig into open pockets among the lily pads.

Fishing was the one common denominator in Jerry's life. He could never remember a time when he did not fish or at least want to fish. Carla was the one woman in his life who understood his passion and shared it with him. But, she could not understand the depths of politics. She could not understand how people vested with political power might crush, even kill, inventors of new technology to keep their financial empires intact. Or, how Jerry could so upset some very big apple carts with his little water powered electric car.

Jerry finished off his last apple from the orchard at the end of Mt. Wolf Road as he methodically hooked bluegill and pumpkinseed sunfish from the pond. The larger fish he slipped on a homemade stringer and released the small fry.

"This is a fine way to spend a day." Jerry thought to himself, alone in the shade of a weeping willow tree.

As the sun was going down, Jerry took his stringer of fat sunfish from the water and mounted his three wheel electric steed. He stopped at the edge of a cornfield and threw three ears of field corn into his back pack. He was going to have a hot meal.

After dark, Largent parked his ElecTrike behind the dry kiln boiler room at the lumberyard and plugged the charger into a nearby outlet. In the boiler room, he found a nearly empty gallon can of denatured alcohol. Jerry dumped the contents outside into the weeds and rinsed the can. He took a small grinder and made three cuts on one side to fabricate a hinged lid.

He took more than a few seconds to hone a razor sharp edge on his fillet knife.

On a slab of wood under the light of a droplight, Jerry filleted out the half dozen sunfish from his stringer. He shucked the ears of corn and snapped each one in half. Into the can went the ears of corn with the filets stacked between. The bloody slab, fish carcasses, and corn husks were disposed of in the burning embers of the boiler firebox. He saved the sunfish bellies in a small Ziploc plastic bag that he had scrounged from a trash can.

Jerry added a little water to the contents of the big rectangular can. He laid the can on top of the firebox and placed a brick on top of the can to hold the lid flap of his homemade crock pot in place.

With his trike on charge and his breakfast simmering, Jerry Largent retired to his mini-barn abode. He still had to wake up before daybreak.

The steaming hot fish fillets and tough field corn made a fine Thursday morning meal but they lacked one important ingredient, seasoning.

"I surely miss Susan's Special Spice." Jerry thought while he consumed the rather bland meal before dawn. In his life as a St. Mary's County elected official, he had used the locally produced seasoning on almost all his meat and seafood but he would have to do without for a while. He could only buy the seasoning from Susan at her bed and breakfast. "No, that is not part of the plan." Jerry realized.

"The long term plan is to head south. The short term plan is to find a cheeseburger."

Chapter 26 A New Messiah

The Thursday morning sunrise found officially deceased Commissioner Jerry Largent beyond the gravel end of Suite Landing Road with a fishing line in Indian Creek. He had cast out a simple bottom rig baited with a tough sunfish belly. This day, his quarry was fat channel catfish that cruise Maryland's estuarine waters.

The trip from the mill along the shoulder of Golden Beach Road was uneventful, but productive. Ten apples from a tree overhanging a side street lay in his back pack. His rod was propped in a small forked tree. While waiting for a cat to bump his bait, Jerry was intent on tuning his guitar.

He had no tuning fork or pitch pipe to establish a standard pitch. He wondered what note the cicadas generally hummed but did not know the answer. He took his best guess with the bottom E string and used that string to set the pitch for the rest of the strings. After a few minutes of adjustment (he had plenty of time), Jerry had the guitar in tune, at least with itself.

During the day, between bites on his cut bait, Jerry recollected many of the standards that he used to play and attempt to sing. He also pulled from his memory bank a few of the original songs that he penned in another place in time before he became involved in politics.

When the rod tip would twitch, Jerry very quickly would stop playing and ease the guitar into the case. He would then pick up the rod and carefully feel for the big bite to set the hook on a cautious catfish. By the end of the day,

Jerry had three large five to six pound channel catfish swimming on a stringer in the creek. He had released half dozen smaller cats.

There was far more meat here than Jerry needed for dinner. He could not share the fillets with his neighbors as he would have done in his previous life. As he released two of the fish from the stringer, he took mercy on the third fish and let that one go too.

"I'd rather have a cheeseburger." Jerry thought. He watched the last fish swim off and he heard a snort come from up the creek.

He looked upstream to see his manatee friend slipping downstream from his freshwater fed pool at the end of the estuary.

"Manny, it's time to head south. Cold weather is coming." Jerry called out from the edge of the water thinking he should take his own advice.

"Now, I'm talking to critters, and myself."

Jerry waved goodbye to the displaced Floridian. He packed up his gear, strapped his guitar case behind the seat of his trike, and headed back to his refuge at the mill. He stopped along the way to pick up some peanut butter crackers from a vending machine to go with an apple for dinner.

"Tomorrow, I am going to talk to someone and eat a cheeseburger." Jerry silently resolved as he bathed from a bucket of hot water in the darkness of the dry kiln boiler room.

The fourth Thursday night of the month is the regular schedule for the monthly meeting of the St. Mary's Republican Club. After a somber moment of silence to remember deceased County Commissioner Jerry Largent, the meeting began with the introduction of the newest member of the club, Buster Butler.

Buster aligned himself as a staunch supporter of Abraham Lincoln and the freedoms secured for all men from the great conflict of the Civil War. Buster made sure that the members were well aware of his residence on his father's farm in Northern St. Mary's County. He did not disclose that he had just become a Republican earlier that week. He asked Commissioner President Doris Gunn-Manning to join him in a rousing rendition of Battle Hymn of the Republic prior to closing his comments.

The entire club joined in on the chorus:

"Glory glory, Hallelujah. Glory glory, Hallelujah."

"Glory glory, Hallelujah. His truth is marching on!"

After the meeting, club members met in the oyster shell parking lot of the Mary's Creek Crab House prior to driving off. This is when the real work of politics is accomplished. Republicans who had formerly divided over grassroots Tea Party issues versus the wealthy special interests found a common bond in this charismatic black businessman from former Commissioner Largent's district.

"Maybe, God has given us a blessing from the great tragedy of Commissioner Largent's demise." Commissioner Gunn-Manning told her loosely assembled audience overlooking the Patuxent River. "Buster Butler would be a great ally on our Board and help us bring those Democratic scalawags in line."

The Republicans cheered. Central Committee members Margaret Miller and Kathleen Knutson warmly hugged each other.

"We must call for a special meeting of the Republican Central Committee on Saturday night." Mrs. Knutson declared.

"Yes, we must!" Mrs. Miller heartily agreed.

While Buster Butler was rising to the status of the new Messiah of the St. Mary's Republican Party, Pennsylvania State Senator Ephraim Stauffer was taking his last breath on his bed in the Harrisburg Hilton Hotel.

State Senator Stauffer was the Republican shoe-in for the upcoming 2012 U.S. Senate position in Pennsylvania. He was also the favored candidate of the Council of 33 who were paving his political trail.

The highly seasoned shrimp creole in the Hilton Ballroom benefit dinner had given him intense heartburn. The nice Asian waiter who served the meal was kind enough to supply the antacid tablets that he had taken. This hard working oriental young man also helped a very dizzy Ephraim Stauffer to his room.

Now, Jung Fang was sitting nearby, patiently waiting for not to be U.S. Senator Ephraim Stauffer to die. The needle in the State Senator's arm and heroin in his bloodstream was enough fodder to feed and fuel the media.

Jung Fang had bigger fish to fry.

Chapter 27 One Choice Cheeseburger

It was the one week anniversary of his death when Jerry Largent awoke to peruse and cruise his neighborhood in the wee morning hours before sunrise.

He was relatively clean and quite lean. His middle age gut had all but disappeared. Though he looked older because of his growing grey beard and shining bald head, Jerry actually felt as healthy and alive as he felt many years ago when he lived a rather carefree existence in the Florida mangroves. He also felt rising internal desires beyond his want for a cheeseburger, but, though he was officially dead, he was still a married man.

The cheeseburger would have to suffice.

Forty two dollars in bills and a couple dollars in change were tucked in the pockets of his cleanest blue jeans as he cruised through the side streets in Charlotte Hall on his motorized senior tricycle.

The front page of the weekend edition of the *County Sentinel* in the commuter parking lot vending machine hinted at an investigation of the wreck involving an on duty Sheriff's car and a teenager from a well-known County family. Jerry kept his change in his pocket. The *Seventh Sun* should hit the street tomorrow.

As Jung Fang was checking out of the Conestoga River Campground with his camper in tow and his electric motorcycle strapped upright in the bed of his Toyota pick-up truck, Jerry Largent was pedaling and motoring north on the hiker biker trail out of St. Mary's County.

He was headed to the great jewel of economic prosperity in Charles County, the neighboring town of Hughesville.

During his first term as a St. Mary's County Commissioner, the Charles County Commissioners who had three Republicans on their five-member Board made a bold business decision. They traded to secure a large parcel of land in Hughesville from the regional electric utility.

This flat open land was adjacent to a combination of the town, the working CSX railroad right-of-way, and an abandoned railroad right-of-way that came from the south. By a quirk of State law, the St. Mary's County Commissioners had been entrusted with the deed for that right-of-way that intruded deep into Charles County.

The Charles County Commissioners floated a State bond issue to build a minor league baseball stadium in the regional center of Southern Maryland.

The huge parking lot hosts thousands of cars full of fans on the weekends while five days a week, the same parking lot is filled with daily commuters catching either a bus to Washington D.C. or a Marc Train to the BWI Airport or Bowie Amtrak station.

Hughesville has transformed from a dying tobacco trading ghost town into a thriving commercial community full of quaint shops and specialty dining bistros. The nearby Harley Davidson dealer has achieved the highest national sales status for five years in a row as affluent Federal government workers in the metro Washington D.C. and Baltimore area take the bus or train into Hughesville and drive home on an American made hog.

Commissioner Jerry Largent's contribution to this economic boom was relatively minor. He recommended the extension of the hiker biker trail to his fellow Republican commissioners who held a majority on the other side of his County Line.

The Democratic commissioners from St. Mary's County were not aware that Commissioner Largent had made this suggestion; otherwise, the request to use the right-of-way would have been D.O.A. Although leery, they allowed for the infrastructure improvements paid by the Charles County board hoping some economic benefit might trickle south.

Jerry Largent spent the day cruising on the trail and walking around the parking lot of the new stadium. Jerry eased up to a big Ford pick-up truck and moved the oversized side mirror to check out his countenance. For the first time since his death a week ago, Jerry could accurately see his reflection. Even he did not recognize himself.

He pulled his red, white, and blue doo rag and dark sunglasses off to get a closer look at this old man he saw in the mirror. Except for the steel blue sparkle of his eyes, Jerry Largent was looking at someone else.

"Good, it's time to hit Hog Heaven." Jerry thought.

Hog Heaven is a local biker bar between the hiker biker trail and old Route 5 that runs through Hughesville. He had never stopped there but he did know it has one hell of a reputation. Hog Heaven is reputed to have the best cheeseburger in all of Southern Maryland.

Jerry Largent was about to find out.

He re-tied his bandana on his head, slapped on his wrap-around welder's sunglasses, mounted his trike, and hit the trail.

It was 2:00 P.M. when Jerry Largent pulled into the back parking lot of the Hog Heaven Bar and Grill. He parked his trike in the empty lot. He cautiously walked in, stopped for a few seconds to adjust to his eyes to the room, and took a seat at the bar. He was the only customer in the place.

"What ya want?" asked the barkeep.

"Cheeseburger." were the first words Jerry had spoken to a person in a week.

"A cheeseburger with lettuce and tomato, ketchup and French fries. No mayo, definitely, no mayo. And a cold ten ounce Bud." Jerry clarified his order.

"Look Bud, I can cover the food but you'll have to roll further south for the ten ounce Budweiser. Will a twelve ounce red and white suit your discriminating taste?" asked the rather satirical bartender.

"Pop a top and bring it on." replied Jerry.

The first sip of the twelve ounce can of Budweiser beer tasted beyond fine as Jerry heard the sound of two motorcycle exhausts rumbling in the back parking lot. The U.S. Marine Viet Nam veteran who was tending bar had more attuned ears than Jerry.

"Wimp bikes." he said.

What neither Jerry or the gruff bartender could see was the two matched custom metal flake painted Harley Sportster bikes that were propped on either side of Jerry's fire engine red senior ElecTrike. One was a solid hot pink color while the other was pearl white with candy purple trim.

The riders were even more stunning.

Jerry watched the veteran's jaw drop as the two riders walked through the door. Largent chose not to look around but focus on the bartender's reaction.

"This seat taken, Greybeard?" as a beautiful blonde model in a tight white leather suit took the seat to the left of him.

"How about this one?" The ravishing black beauty in black leather took the seat to his right.

"Ladies choice." Largent said thinking this sure beat swimming with a manatee.

"I'm Peaches and she's Sativa." explained the Nordic bombshell to Jerry.

"Peaches and Herb?" Largent questioned.

"Yeah, something like that," The Nubian queen laughed. "There's a lot that lies beneath the surface of that mangy grey beard."

And from both directions, both women kissed him on both his cheeks at the same time.

"And what's your name, Greybeard." Peaches asked.

" Greybeard." Largent replied.

Both women laughed.

"And what are you having?" asked Sativa.

"Cheeseburger" Jerry Greybeard said and clarified again. "Cheeseburger with lettuce and tomato, ketchup and French fries. No mayo, definitely no mayo. And a cold Budweiser beer. They only have twelve ounce in the can."

"Sounds good to us. We'll have the same," Sativa spoke for both riders. "Put Greybeard's tab on our bill."

He started to protest but decided to go with the flow. Greybeard nodded his acceptance and said, "Ladies choice."

The awestruck bartender gently placed their beers on the counter.

"That's a pretty hot ride you've got tethered out back." Peaches said.

Before Jerry could reply to the sarcasm he sensed, Sativa cut in.

"Those Optima Blue top batteries must give you a lot more range. Are you running a series wound or permanent magnet motor?"

"Yes, I figure I can roll for fifty miles before recharging and the drive is a 400 watt permanent magnet motor." Jerry replied.

"Neo-dymnium boron magnets?" she asked.

"No, it's a Chinese marvel of old tech simplicity. It's hardly a Harley. You sure know a lot about EVs." Jerry noted.

"Yes, I majored in engineering at MIT. I'm the brains of the outfit." said Sativa.

"But, I'm the heart. My degree in Sociology came from Florida State." Peaches chimed in.

"And what are you two doing in this neck of the woods?" Jerry asked, somewhat embarrassed by the rhetorical sound of his query.

"We just finished a photo shoot across the street at Hughesville Harley Davidson and are heading to another modeling gig up the coast in Boston," explained Peaches.

The burgers and fries arrived in unison. Patiently, Jerry waited for the ladies to begin their meals before he took his first bite.

Hot cheddar cheese blended with fresh ground beef to produce an ecstatic taste sensation in his mouth as he was sandwiched between two of the finest examples of feminine pulchritude that he had ever witnessed in any of his lifetimes.

Jerry Largent really was in Hog Heaven.

Chapter 28 Deal of a Lifetime

"That's a fine looking pinky ring." Sativa noted the solid silver ring on the little finger of Greybeard's right hand as he savored the center bite of his big burger.

Jerry replied, "It's got a story."

"Tell us, please," both gals pled.

"Sorry girls, it's an all-night tale."

"Then you can roll to New England with us. We'll be happy to share our company if you'll share your story." Peaches spoke for the two of them.

"My trike will never keep up with your bikes." Jerry observed.

Sativa replied, "Our Sportsters are only for bopping around town. We keep them in an enclosed trailer that we pull with a Dodge dually crew cab with the Cummins diesel. It's parked at Hughesville Harley. Your trike can ride in the bed. You can bunk with us. Can you shift a manual tranny?"

"Do fish swim?" Jerry answered her question with another question. "But my license to drive is long gone."

"Bet there's another story there." pondered Peaches.

"Not one I'm telling." Greybeard replied.

"The deal still stands." Sativa said. "You can still drive at night and escort us during the day. We'll cover room and board and fifty bucks a day in cash for your companionship. It should keep the young hustlers off our backs and you might enjoy the company."

"Best deal I've been offered in this lifetime." Greybeard dryly observed. "But I'm headed south. I'm leaving tomorrow."

"Well, we might catch you on the return trip in the fall. We've got shoots along the coast in Norfolk, Charleston, Daytona Beach, and Miami before a little wintertime R and R in Key West." said Sativa as she paid the entire bill and tip with her credit card. Both girls again kissed him on his stubbly cheeks as they rose from their seats and left the bar.

The perplexed bartender and Jerry heard both bikes rumble into the distance.

Jerry reached into his pocket and put two bucks on the bar. "One more Bud for the road, please."

With his trike plugged in behind the dry kiln boiler room, Jerry went right to sleep in his mini-barn soon after dark.

This was to be a slow Friday night in the world where Commissioner Jerry Largent once lived.

There were no weekend parties scheduled at the Canoe Creek Bar and Grill. The Democratic network in St. Mary's County was in no mood for celebration.

His assassin, Arthur Ching a.k.a. Jung Fang, was unhooking his camper at a Massachusetts campground in Sturbridge. He was targeting a Congressman from New England to continue his mission of Chinese retribution.

Commissioner President Doris Gunn-Manning was on the phone contacting Republican Central Committee members to support Buster Butler as the appointed replacement for Commissioner Jerry Largent.

Carla Largent was in deep dream sleep playing with her departed daughter but Jerry had yet to show up to join them.

Jerry Largent woke up at 3:00 A.M. on Saturday morning.

He drove the fully charged bike from the kiln to quickly slip inside the portable shed. Under the light from his single headlight, Jerry packed up his gear hiding his pistol deep within his back pack with six remaining apples located for easy access. He kept a couple dollars' worth of change and his remaining forty dollars of paper money in his pockets. The change jar jingled in his back pack.

His guitar was in its tough case strapped behind the seat of his trike atop a small tarp that was folded over his 24 volt plug-in charger and held by bungee cords between the two rear wheels. Jerry pushed his ElecTrike out the door and locked the outside lock one last time. He hit the street.

Jerry Largent watched from the shadows as Bardog Nelson filled the new yellow vending machine for the *Seventh Sun* weekly newspaper at the Charlotte Hall commuter parking lot. When Bardog's pick-up truck left, Largent slipped four quarters into the machine and grabbed a paper.

The headline read: "Drunken Sheriff Mows Down Seventh Son".

Though he should have been rolling south, Jerry Largent stood under the parking lot security light transfixed by the article he was reading.

Punkin Nelson pulled no punches as she reported how Sheriff Chuck Hall had gotten drunk at a Democratic party hosted by Commissioners Alvey, Lyons, and Leonard in celebration of the death of Commissioner Jerry Largent. The morbid event was held in the County owned bar and grill at the Canoe Neck Golf Course. And, the taxpayers of St. Mary's County had footed bill to the tune of $9,426.84!

On his way home in his Sheriff's car, a very inebriated Sheriff Hall slipped across the center line and plowed into Jimmy Guy who was traveling back to his family's farm in the Seventh District from freshman orientation in College Park. Jimmy had secured a full four year athletic scholarship to the University of Maryland. Jimmy Guy was instantly killed. The State Police recorded Sheriff Hall with a blood alcohol level of .16 which is twice the legal limit.

"Looks like Sheriff Hall's days are numbered." thought Jerry Largent.

Though he did not have access to the Internet, dwihitparade.com also coldly assessed the actions of St. Mary's County Sheriff Chuck Hall: "Boozing Sheriff Slides Across Centerline to Kill Star Center Fielder".

The two beers that Jerry Largent had consumed the day before had long passed through his kidneys when he was rolling from St. Mary's County and through Charles County on the shoulder of Route 6 in the darkness.

Driving a dimly lit three wheeler down a rural road at night is not as easy as it might seem.

Avoiding road kill on a four wheel vehicle is a simple matter of straddling the carcass. It is a lot harder to straddle a dead body with a wheel in the middle.

Also, possums are serious obstacles at night to riders of senior trikes. Under a car wheel, they go thump. When thumped by a tricycle they snap back with their jaws. Then there are unseen things that fly by, probably bats.

Jerry Largent was glad the sun was coming up as he turned left off Route 6 onto Penns Hill Road. Traversing that shoulder less road especially rolling down the winding steep incline was a major accomplishment of survival when he came to the stop sign on Route 234.

The shoulders on both Route 234 and Route 301 made for easy traveling until he came to his first major real obstacle in his journey south, the Harry Nice Bridge that crossed the Potomac River.

Around 9:00 A.M., Jerry Largent found himself stuck at the truck stop half a mile before the Potomac River looking for a way across a bridge with no pedestrian or bicycle access lane.

He purchased a black magic marker at the truck stop convenience store and marked on a white cardboard box lid: "Old Man Needs Ride for Trike in Pick-up Truck". He opened his guitar case, pulled out his guitar, and put the sign in along with a few dollars and some spare change. Jerry strapped on his guitar and started singing the few songs he knew.

It was not long before a matronly black woman in a Toyota Yaris tossed two quarters into his case after he performed a rough rendition of "Youngblood" by the Coasters.

Chapter 29 One Hit Wonder

In his former life, Jerry Largent was a pretty good bass plucker. In his present incarnation, he left a lot to be desired as a street singer with an acoustic guitar.

With a repertoire of about a dozen familiar songs, he didn't have much to choose from to coax a bit of change from passing motorists entering and leaving the truck stop restaurant/convenience store.

However, his political savvy came in handy matching the tune with the tipper. Older country folks were responsive to songs from classic country artists like Hank Williams Sr. or Randy Travis. The senior black audience would flip a quarter for a Chuck Berry tune or an old R&B standard. All the seniors, regardless of skin color, loved Buddy Holly. "Maybe Baby" followed by "That'll be the Day" became his one/two punch for pulling a quarter out of a tight pocket or purse.

Middle age people always turned an ear to a Jimmy Buffett song or a Sixties anthem like "For What It's Worth" by Buffalo Springfield. But, he lacked any insight into the musical interests of the young people who gave the grey bearded old man a wide berth.

He had almost five additional dollars in change and two more dollar bills in his guitar case when a young man in an old Dodge pick-up truck pulled into the parking lot around lunchtime.

Jerry eyed the potential ride carefully. The half-ton Dodge must have been a Seventies model. The simple body lines were a little softer than the next generation square body Dodge pick-ups. It was painted primer grey and had a blue solar panel mounted on the roof. Yes, a bright blue solar panel! And, hanging across the gun rack in the rear window was a light to medium action fishing rod with a Penn Gold spinning reel. It looked to be the same reel model that Jerry had stored in his back pack.

Largent knew he only had one cast to hook this kindred spirit.

From deep in his memory bank, he pulled an original song he had written years about his own father and every fisherman's fantasy.

His George Thorogood style lead intro stopped the young man long enough for Jerry to belt out the 12 bar blues in A:

"Daddy was a captain and he rolled upon the sea."

"Till he met a landlocked lady and they had a family."

"Now, he's given up the ocean and he's working in a mill."

"Although he's paid his dues, he got to pay the bills."

"He moved his boat up to a river that runs down to the Bay."

"And on most any weekend, he is headed out to play."

"Well Mama used to scream and Mama used to yell,"

"When Daddy would go fishing and make her cooler smell."

"She wouldn't cook his catch. She didn't care at all."

"She'd curse his nasty bass and go buy Mrs. Paul's."

"Now, his stringer comes home empty, Daddy has no fresh fillets."

"But we know he's been fishing 'cause his fingers smell like bait."

"Has Daddy got a mermaid? Has Daddy got a mermaid?"

"Does a wild water woman got him bouncing and bumping on the Bay?"

"Has Daddy got a mermaid? Or, do his fish get away?"

After he picked the simple lead break, Jerry fed out a little more line to snag his likely chauffeur who had stayed through the first half of the song and was listening closely:

"My friends have tried to tell me something fishy's going on."

"He's been leaving after dark and coming home before the dawn."

"He's been rolling on the river. He's been bumping on the Bay."

"They can't see what he's been doing without the light of day."

"He sealed the cabin curtains and locked the inside lock."

"And on the calmest day, his boat is rocking at the dock."

"So, I played the good detective, though I didn't have a clue."

"I guess I was too young to know what Daddy was up to."

"I grabbed my brightest flashlight and I snuck out of my bed."

"And went down to the bank, down by the river's edge."

"When I heard my Daddy's diesel, I turned on that floodlight beam."

"Now, I know you won't believe it but I'll tell you what I seen."

"My Daddy's got a mermaid. My Daddy's got a mermaid."

"A wild water woman's got him bouncing and bumping on the Bay."

"My Daddy's got a mermaid. But, his mermaid's got..."

Jerry was poised to set the hook as he moved the descending final blues riff to end the song. The young man listened intently for the last word:

"Legs!!!"

The young truck driving, solar powered fisherman grabbed his gut laughing. Jerry clinched the punch line with an octave lower bluesy "Oh yeah!" and picked the obligatory triplet blues lead tag to officially close the potential platinum hit single.

"Old Man, I was going to give you a ride, but I'd like to offer you lunch as well." said the young driver of the old Dodge truck.

"Best offer I've had all day. Thanks." said Jerry. He packed up his guitar, stuffed his loot in his pocket, and joined his driver at a dining booth.

"They call me Country," said the dark haired young man.

"Just call me Jarvis," Jerry thought Jarvis was a pretty good spur of the moment name.

"Is Jarvis your first or last name?" Country asked.

"Either, neither, or both. Kind of like Country. Good enough for now," was Jerry's cryptic reply.

"OK by me, let's have lunch."

Country ordered a rib-eye steak sandwich and Jarvis ordered a pancake breakfast with scrambled eggs, bacon, and sausage. He ordered an iced tea, no sugar, while Country requested a Coke with light ice.

"They always put too little soda and too much ice in the drinks. I want my money's worth."

Jarvis asked what Country did for a living.

"I have a regional route for installing lightning rods. My territory includes Richmond, Washington D.C. and Baltimore. That's enough to keep me working steady as long as the weather will cooperate."

"Bad weather keeps you off the roofs?" asked Jarvis.

"No, just the opposite, bad weather gets me work. A good lightning storm can move a lot of jobs my way. People don't think ahead much anymore except for a few old timers." said Country. "I've got a couple weeks' worth of work in front of me from the big storm that pounded Colonial Beach about a month ago. I could use some help. Mainly, I need a gofer. You know, gofer this and gofer that, to bring stuff from the truck to the base of the ladder. I can hoist with a line to the roof. There's a room, hot meals, and twenty bucks a day if you're up for it."

Compared to the gravy deal offered by Peaches and Sativa yesterday afternoon this gig was the pits. "Let me think about it. I really need to roll south." Jarvis decided to keep his options open.

Jarvis was served first and he dug right in. He asked for extra butter that he spread evenly between all three hotcakes and heaped the syrup on thick.

When he finished his meal, there was not a bit of food, trace of syrup, or crumb left.

"Would you like a piece of pie for dessert?" the waitress asked.

"No, thank you, I'm done," said Jarvis.

"Me too."

Country paid the bill and put a couple dollars on the table. Jarvis added a couple more from the stash in his pocket. She was a nice waitress.

In the parking lot, Country rearranged his tools and the folding ladder in the bed of his truck and dropped the rear gate. He and Jarvis lifted the ElecTrike over the gate and pushed it forward. Country closed the gate. Jarvis threw his back pack in and got ready to stow his guitar case as well.

"No, we'll make room for her in the cab of the truck with us." Country offered.

After paying the toll and crossing the river into Virginia, the young lightning rod installer asked Jarvis to open up the guitar case. Country reached into a cigar box and pulled out a Marine Band blues harp in the key of E.

"Now let's tune that git-box up right," said Country. "It's a little on the flat side."

Chapter 30 Country Bucks

The Council of 33 had no idea of the threat to their economic power base that might come from an unlikely pair who were picking guitar and blowing blues harp rolling down Route 301 in Virginia.

The Council had bigger worries.

The death of Pennsylvania State Senator Ephraim Stauffer was being widely publicized as a drug overdose. The Council knew better. They had positioned Ephraim for political greatness. Their own blood analysis from the autopsy revealed that this was a professional hit. Their investigation pointed to an unknown Asian waiter.

The Asian part of the equation is what they feared the most.

As of a week ago, all contact with the Chinese representative of the Red and Green Societies had been severed. The envoy sent by the Council had simply disappeared. The Council was being hung out to dry by the Chinese and they were not sure of the reason.

They feared they would lose more members, one cut at a time.

Gus Herald, their dirty business consultant in South Florida, was not worthy to be a member of the Council. He was a hired gun who hired guns. Gus had taken care of the Bird Flu Treaty violation that former Commissioner Jerry Largent and his water powered car represented. No one in the world other than China was allowed to promote viable innovative free energy technology especially not an elected official.

Gus assured the Council that Jerry Largent was officially dead. Fast Freddy was sent his last payment directly to his bank account after the bumpkin Sheriff closed the case and Gus greased the investigatory network. Sheriff Hall's other problem was related to stupidity. He could pay his own price for that blunder.

As confident as Gus portrayed himself to the Council over the phone, he had some nagging doubt over the results of the Largent water car bombing plot. Fast Freddy was not returning Gus's calls.

Assistant Fire Marshall Stephen Waterford paid Mrs. Carla Largent three hundred dollars scrap metal price for the burned out MR2 in her driveway. For another hundred bucks, he contracted a roll-back tow truck to haul it to his own garage for some off duty study. Down the street, he noticed another car being towed away. A later check of the St. Mary's Sheriff's Department records showed the car had been rented to Fredrico Fernandez of Ft. Lauderdale and abandoned in Golden Beach.

"Everybody knows a little bit about something, but no one knows everything about everything." Jarvis told his young driver in a break between songs while they rode to Colonial Beach. "Like that solar panel on your roof. What's the purpose for that?"

"I've got it wired to a heavy duty battery under the hood that powers a hydrogen booster and a cold water vapor injector. You know anything about that?" Country asked.

"Well, maybe a little bit." Jarvis figured not to play his whole hand.

Country explained the basic principles.

"It works something like this: Water in a reservoir cell is broken down into hydrogen and oxygen from electricity that comes free by converting photons from the sun. The hydrogen/gas mix is fed into the fuel/air stream to make a better burn. The water vapor offsets the faster flame speed of the hydrogen/oxygen gas mix while expanding as steam to give more power. This is a carbureted truck so I had to drop the jet size a bit and retard the timing a little but the old slant six is getting almost thirty miles per gallon. Also, the exhaust is cleaner than what comes out of a car with a catalytic converter."

"What kind of output are you pumping from your electrolyzer?" Jarvis questioned.

"Two liters per minute through a Double Six Pack Hot Stack stainless cell."

"What electrolyte are you using?" Jarvis asked.

"Sodium Hydroxide but I'm running low. It's hard to find."

"I've got an off the shelf source across the river." Jarvis noted.

Country smiled and said, "It looks like you know maybe more than a little bit about hydrogen boosters."

"Maybe so, grab that harp in E. I think I remember the words to Folsom Prison Blues." Jarvis cranked out the opening riff and pulled the Johnny Cash song out of his hat which happened to be a red, white, and blue doo rag. Country's harmonica playing sounded good. Damned good. And, the boy had a strong tenor voice. They made a pretty good duo.

Country stopped at the Colonial Beach Sleep Inn to secure a room for the next two weeks.

"Well, you ready to roll south or pick up a couple week's work?" asked Country.

"If you'll add some country bucks to the pot, I'll go fer the gofer gig."

"OK, I'll bite. What's country bucks?" Country asked.

Jarvis explained, "You stop in a Country bar with a guitar and a decent voice and people give you money. I've got the guitar. You've got the voice. The Lucky Strike Saloon is a good place to shop for our first gig tonight."

"I've been singing karaoke since I was a teenager and no one offered to throw money at me." said Country.

"You should have learned to play guitar," quipped Jarvis.

Country paid for a room with twin beds. Jarvis took a long hot shower. It was the first full bathing experience he had in over a week.

In their room, Jarvis and Country went over a long list of songs and keys that they could play in together. They had at least three dozen songs they could jointly cover and could probably fumble through more requests. Jarvis took his magic marker and wrote the word, TIPS, on a piece of white cardboard which he put in the guitar case.

They both had a big steak dinner in the Lucky Strike Saloon. While they were having cold draft beer after the meal, one of the guys at the bar noted the guitar case beside Jarvis. "Can you play that thing or you just carry it around for looks?"

Jarvis opened the case which he left on the floor. He propped up the TIPS sign and strapped on his guitar. He whipped out the intro to "Three Steps" by Lynrd Skynrd. Country kicked in with the vocals. They traded lead licks on guitar and blues harp. Together, they sang the chorus. When they ended the song, the whole place erupted in applause. Instead of running for the door, Jarvis and

Country kicked into "Jambalaya" and dozens more songs. They never stopped playing till midnight.

They closed out the evening with an acoustic version of "Wonderful Tonight" by Eric Clapton. Jarvis latched his case full of money and his guitar tightly shut. When the crowd thinned, the bartender offered them fifty bucks each to do the same gig later that day on Sunday evening from 7 to 10 P.M. Country agreed but Jarvis insisted that the TIPS sign stay posted. The Old Man knew where the real money was.

Jarvis and Country slept well through Sunday morning. When he awoke in a clean warm bed with the air-conditioner blowing cool air, Jarvis had almost forgotten how hard that mini-barn floor had been. He got up and counted the bills and change scattered through his guitar case.

Two hundred and fourteen dollars and fifty cents was their take for their first Colonial Beach Saturday Night. Jarvis was ready to trade his work boots for a pair of Tony Lamas.

Chapter 31 Lightning Rod Revelations

Country could not believe that he had made a hundred and seven dollars and twenty five cents singing and playing his harmonicas in a country bar.

"Don't let this go to your head but you're a natural born singer. You've got the gift of melody. It flows from your voice and through the harps you wail on. Problem is you need a picker to put the rhythm underneath the lead line." Jarvis advised his duet partner. "I've got the picking down pat but I barely carry a tune in a bucket with my voice. Between the two of us, we make one good combo but in two weeks our day will be done. So, let's clean up our act, leave this town with a few bucks in our pockets and get a little wiser along the way. The Sunday afternoon crowd at the Lucky Strike will be tougher because they are not well liquored up before we start."

Jarvis and Country spent the afternoon polishing songs, smoothing out harmonies, and working out the proper cross harp key combinations so Country could shine without fumbling through his cigar box for the right harmonica. Jarvis also showed Country some simple chords on the guitar and how they fit with the melodies he sang. Before long, Country would have the whole package and Jarvis would be long gone.

They both had seafood platters prior to playing. The Sunday afternoon duo was musically far less rowdy but much more professional. Jarvis and Country played without a break till after 10 P.M. The crowd was not as large as the night before but it was a very good mix for a Sunday evening. The owner of the bar was happy and offered them five hundred bucks to cover the coming Friday, Saturday, and Sunday nights.

There was a hundred and twenty bucks of tips in his guitar case that evening. Jarvis divided the cash with Country and went to bed early.

Country cut Jarvis no slack when they started work on Monday morning. By 9:00 A.M., Country was on top of the first roof of a small cottage on a back creek lot. Jarvis hoofed the lightning rods, ground wires, and tools from the truck and tied them to the line that Country pulled above.

The hard part was driving the ten foot long ground rods into the soil but Country had a trick. He had built an electric gear driven drill with a six foot long one inch bit that plugged into his solar powered battery under the hood of his truck. Free energy from the sun took the ground rod six feet into the ground. A little water in the hole, a simple technique of slipping the rod up and down, a few taps with a small sledge and the rod was deep in the ground.

By the third installation after lunch, Jarvis pretty much knew the routine to follow. Once he was ahead of his goffering, he climbed to the top of the ladder to watch Country complete the rooftop installation.

As Country mounted the pointed rods along the peak of the roof, he asked Jarvis, "This is called a Franklin rod, do you know why?"

Jarvis was to go to the head of the class. "Because Ben Franklin invented the lightning rod."

"Well very good, but did you know that there is more energy in a lightning bolt than the scientists can account for?" Country knew he had stumped his star student.

"Of course there is. And, did you know you could tap that extra energy to make more than enough hydrogen to run your truck without any gasoline at all?" Jarvis put him in his place.

In shock, Country dropped his hammer that slid down the roof. The momentum carried it over the gutter and gravity pulled it to the ground. Jarvis climbed down the ladder, retrieved the hammer, climbed up the ladder, and placed it in Country's hand.

"But you can't control lightning, Franklin learned that." Country said.

"Of course you can, Nikola Tesla knew better." Jarvis explained. "Every day, you control lightning in the cylinders of your Dodge slant six engine through the spark plugs."

"How do you think guys like Herman Andersen, Andrija Puharich, Stan Meyers, and most recently, Jerry Largent, ran their cars on water?" Jarvis was throwing his ace trump card.

Country slipped but caught himself by grabbing the roof peak, "Largent! Did you know Jerry Largent? He's famous on the Internet. He was assassinated by the oil companies!"

"Is that what they're saying?" Jarvis thought but he said, "Maybe, a little bit. Now, I'm going below before you fall off the roof. We'll talk later. We got a whole two weeks."

This was their last job of the day and Country was full of questions, some of which Jarvis needed to avoid. Jarvis diverted the issue by giving Country his guitar and sketching out chord diagrams on the back of an old placemat. While Country practiced through the evening, Jarvis asked if he could use Country's laptop computer to cruise the Internet.

"No problem. Stay off the porn sites. I don't want you having a heart attack over my computer," joked Country.

At a picnic table overlooking the Potomac River, Jarvis Googled his former name and the media reports. Pretty much all of them attributed the death of Commissioner Jerry Largent to a tragic accident caused by his dangerous invention. The *Seventh Sun* website was not on-line yet but he had already read the one investigative report by Punkin Nelson in her first issue. She was the only one who came close to the truth that even he did not even know completely.

He slipped in as a guest to the Internet water fuel forums. The general consensus there was Jerry Largent had joined Stan Meyers in the legendary status of another inventor snuffed out by corporate oil interests.

Somewhat proud of leaving the world as a legend, Jarvis fell asleep as Country was picking the two-four bass line and strumming the C chord to "Digging up Bones" by Randy Travis. The boy was definitely a natural. With a little help, Country could be a legend as well, a living legend.

While Jarvis and Country plugged away on Tuesday morning installing lightning rods in Colonial Beach, the St. Mary's County Commissioners were moving ahead with their agenda in Leonardtown. Commissioner Largent was marked deceased in the attendance portion of their minutes but the rest of them were at the table.

Over the weekend, Commissioner President Doris Gunn-Manning had read the report in the *Seventh Sun* about her fellow commissioners' party to which she was not invited.

She chaired the meeting professionally according to Roberts Rules of Order but curtly according to her own opinion of her fellow commissioners. She would not be attending those secret meetings in Virginia anymore. She had been told the Colonial Beach meetings were cancelled.

Commissioner President Gunn-Manning closed the meeting before lunch and went home.

The three Democratic Commissioners organized for their meeting with St. Mary's County States Attorney Reginald U. Rhinehart III, a fellow Democrat who had not caught the party fever that followed the loss of Commissioner Largent.

They would have liked to meet at their old haunt in the County owned Canoe Creek Bar and Grill but there was too much potential scrutiny especially with Punkin Nelson snooping around.

Colonial Beach was a safer option. Even States Attorney Rhinehart agreed with Commissioner Drake Alvey that a meeting held in Virginia was exempt from the requirements of the St. Mary's Open Meetings Act.

The day went smoothly for the two lightning rod installers. Country sang his songs on the roof as Jarvis eased the ground rods into the soil after delivering the installation equipment to be raised. After they had completed four houses that day, they enjoyed dinner at the Lucky Strike Saloon.

A rumble echoed across the Potomac that Jarvis was very familiar with. He could not translate higher pitched melodies like Country could but he recognized the monotone roar that was heading their way. Jarvis looked out the back window overlooking the Potomac River to see the St. Mary's County yacht "Bottoms Up" pulling up to the Lucky Strike Saloon docks.

Commissioner James Lyons worked the helm while Commissioner Drake Alvey handled the lines. They made a pretty good captain and mate. It was obvious they were familiar to this routine.

They carried their cans of ten ounce Budweiser beer down the pier and entered the private backroom extension of the Lucky Strike Saloon that was built over the Potomac River.

Jarvis kept his head low and said not a word to Country while he consumed his meal and chewed on the situation. A few minutes later, Commissioner Kenny Leonard and States Attorney Reginald U. Rhinehart III walked past their booth. They eased though the rear door of the restaurant and entered the backroom as well.

Feigning indigestion, Jarvis left Country for the evening. He walked out the front door of the Lucky Strike. Jarvis moved close to the side of the building and back around over the planks mounted to pilings that supported the backroom over the river. He moved in close to an open window of the backroom and sat down beside it clutching his stomach. His eyes were closed but his ears were wide open.

"Look boys, the Sheriff is going to take a plea bargain and resign. That's going to take the heat off you for a bit. But, you've got to unload the bar and grill. Bid it out. The public is hot enough over your foolish drunken party. You may be lame ducks but we need to keep our boys in place. Who knows what the damned Republicans might screw up." said States Attorney Rhinehart III.

"Don't worry Reggie, we will soon control the St. Mary's Republican Party." said Commissioner Alvey.

"I don't even want to know!" said the States Attorney. "Just watch your butts!"

"That's the plan." said Commissioner Leonard. "Now, bring on the food and more beer for everyone."

Jarvis returned to the Sleep Inn and printed a simple message with his magic marker on the back of a Lucky Strike Saloon placemat. Before he went to work on Wednesday, he bought a stamped envelope at the Colonial Beach Post Office and addressed it to the *Seventh Sun* newspaper.

The note he put into the envelope and sent read:

ON TUESDAY NIGHT, CHECK OUT THE MEETING IN THE BACKROOM OF THE LUCKY STRIKE SALOON IN COLONIAL BEACH. OBSERVE WHO IS THERE AND WHERE THEY ARE.
Best Regards,
A Concerned Taxpayer.

Chapter 32 One Fine Fishing Tip

On Thursday evening, Jarvis and Country were croaker fishing off the Colonial Beach public pier with their matching Penn Gold spinning reels when a single shot blew Congressman Norton Sweeney's head apart in the posh Boston Patriots Inn dining room. The Council of 33 had lost another member of their elite network.

Jung Fang folded his rifle and scope into a tote bag and silently drove away on his electric motorcycle. This was his third assassination of an elected official in three weeks. Arthur Ching already had his advance reservation for a campground in New York. His Chinese masters were sending a not so subtle message.

Country had been coming along well with his guitar lessons. He and Jarvis were prepped to play the weekend at the Lucky Strike but Country was not ready for a solo act, yet.

"Would you like to run across the river on Saturday to pick up some more caustic soda for your hydrogen booster?" Jarvis asked.

"Good idea, maybe I could check out some guitars. About time I got my own." said the upcoming Country legend.

Country and Jarvis had one fine Friday night performing at the Lucky Strike Saloon. The word had gotten out around town. The girls came out to check out the new boy on the block and dozens of electric golf carts were parked outside. The old timers enjoyed the classic country standards that Jarvis could pull from under his bandana.

On Saturday morning, Country and Jarvis divided over two hundred dollars in tips and headed across the Potomac River Bridge to run some errands.

First stop was in the town of LaPlata. Chesapeake Music is a small store that carries quality new and used instruments at reasonable prices. Jarvis did not know the owner which made it safe for him to enter. He recommended that Country pick an acoustic guitar that felt and sounded good to him. There were plenty of Gibson, Taylor, Martin, and other fine brands for Country to choose from as Jarvis left the store and hit the street.

Jarvis walked down to the courthouse where his wife still worked. It was the weekend. No one was around. He took out his keys that he was carrying for no reason and etched: JERRY LOVES CARLA on the trunk of an old beech tree with the key that once unlocked his MR2. He rubbed his black magic marker into the cuts to emphasize the letters and returned to the music store.

Country had chosen an old used Epiphone guitar made in Kalamazoo that he paid a hundred dollars for including the case.

Jarvis smiled.

"Great minds really do think alike, but I just know a little bit," Country wryly observed.

The next stop was an Amish dry goods store on a gravel lane off of Route 6. There, Country picked up a whole quart of pure sodium hydroxide for five bucks. Though it is not usually found in retail stores, sodium hydroxide is a necessary commodity in self-sufficient households for making soap.

In Charlotte Hall, Jarvis asked Country to stop by the commuter parking lot to pick up a newspaper. The Washington Post carried a big front page story about the assassination of Congressman Norton Sweeney by an unknown assailant.

"Well, it couldn't have been the guy who tried to kill me," thought Jarvis. He did not know how wrong he was.

Locally, the *Seventh Sun* weekly in the yellow newspaper box had grabbed the scoop again:

"Sheriff Hall to Resign - Buster Butler Recommended for North County Commissioner"

Jarvis purchased his third issue of the *Seventh Sun* and directed Country to the town of Benedict which is in Charles County on the Patuxent River.

"Turn right here off of Route 231. Now turn right again and follow this street all the way to the end at the Benedict Pier and Restaurant parking lot." said Jerry. "Park at this boat ramp and look across. Do you see a single crème yellow house among all of the red brick and white houses along the shoreline in Golden Beach?"

"Yes, it sticks out like a sore thumb." said Country.

"That's where Commissioner Jerry Largent used to live. Now, here's the deal. What would you say if Largent had made another electrolyzer that no one but I know about and you could put your hands on it?" Jarvis said.

"I'd show it to the world." promised Country breathlessly.

"Could you wait till I e-mail you or at least a year to do so?" said Jarvis.

"If that's the deal."

"Yes, that's the deal"

"Then count me in." said Country.

"Your word is good enough for me. Look across the creek on the porch of that crème yellow house. See that black barbeque grill?"

Country nodded in agreement.

"Underneath the grill is a propane gas tank that has had the bottom cut out. Inside the hollow shell is a two circuit high/low voltage electrolyzer that pumps the same output Jerry needed to run his ten horsepower generator. It is essentially the exact device he used without the cold water vapor injection unit but it also has an AC to DC converter that allowed him to plug it into his house circuit to fuel his grill." said Jarvis.

"You can slip across the creek in a canoe from here at the edge of dark fishing the edge of the shore for white perch with the spinning rig you've got hanging behind us. A black headed beetle spin with a white body is a deadly combo. After dark, tie up to the dock and disconnect the tank with an adjustable wrench. No one will miss it. Jerry's wife is scheduled to teach Spanish at the community college every Thursday from seven to nine P.M. for this fall semester." Jarvis instructed.

"How do you know so much about Jerry Largent?" asked his incredulous young driver.

"Maybe, I know more than a little bit but you know enough for now. Now, let's stop at that little tackle shop across the Route 231 Pax River Bridge before we go home."

Jarvis went inside the shop and was soon back in the truck. He flipped a small cellophane package into the cigar box of Marine Band harmonicas that Country always carried. Country resisted his initial curiosity and drove back to Colonial Beach.

When he opened the box to grab his first blues harp that evening during their Saturday night gig, Country saw the clear package that held a black headed beetle spin with a white body.

Chapter 33 a New Dawn

Country and Jarvis had a great weekend. They raked in over five hundred dollars each in pay and tips and were booked for one last three day gig at the bar in Colonial Beach, Virginia.

The Council of 33 was not doing nearly as well. They could not understand why their Chinese counterparts who oversaw the Red and Green Societies were knocking off Council members at the rate of one elected official per week. Their only retribution was to release the extremely virulent strain of the Bird Flu virus they had engineered but the Chinese had confiscated all the available vaccine which was securely stored in Central China.

The remaining lightning rod installations were moving smoothly. Jarvis was a good gofer. Late Tuesday afternoon, he took his ElecTrike and guitar for a ride while Country practiced with his own guitar in their air-conditioned motel room.

Jarvis parked the trike under a big poplar tree that had a good shady view of the Lucky Strike Saloon and docks. He pulled out his guitar and picked a few tunes while waiting for the show to begin.

Bardog Nelson's truck was first to arrive in the parking lot. Punkin got out of the driver's side. She had a big scarf over her head and dark sunglasses on. She looked around and walked into the restaurant. Not long after, Jarvis heard the rumble of the County yacht as Commissioners Alvey and Lyons pulled up to the dock. Then, Commissioner Leonard's Town Car chauffeured

States Attorney Reginald U. Rhinehart III into the parking lot. They went into the restaurant.

It was like experiencing déjà vu and watching a predictable movie when Jarvis saw Punkin ease out the restaurant and creep across the pier planks beside the backroom building over the Potomac River to the same window that Jarvis had eavesdropped through a week ago.

Punkin had only one shot. She jumped in front of the window and snapped their photo. She then ran like hell for Bardog's pick-up. Jarvis never saw a short fat woman run so fast. She had left in a cloud of dust as the three dumbfounded commissioners and Reggie were just stumbling out the door. Jarvis laughed all the way back to the Sleep Inn on his electric tricycle. He only wished he could be around to purchase the fourth edition of the *Seventh Sun*.

On Thursday night, Jung Fang put a knife through the throat of New York Congresswoman Wilma Harvey while she slept. The Chinese were not going to be accused of sexual discrimination.

The CeeJay Duo was finishing up their last gig at the Lucky Strike Saloon that weekend. Country and Jarvis had finished up all the previously contracted lightning rod installations plus picked up and completed a half dozen more from local word of mouth references.

They easily rolled through their sets on Friday and Saturday nights. On Sunday night, Jarvis handed his guitar over to Country at 9:30 P.M. Country finished the last half hour of the evening singing and playing on his own.

"The boy's a natural." Jarvis told a fellow redneck at the bar as he ordered another beer.

Back in their room. They split up their last weekend proceeds. Again, each of them had over five hundred dollars cash to add to their savings.

Jarvis asked to check out the Internet news on Country's computer. The *Seventh Sun* newspaper website was up. The front page picture featured three very surprised St Mary's County Commissioners and a stunned States Attorney. The caption above read: "Three Stooge Commissioners and Stupid States Attorney Caught in Open Meetings Violation".

Punkin Nelson got the whole story which she accurately reported. Although most of the Lucky Strike Saloon is in Virginia, the backroom, which at one time housed slot machines, is over the Potomac River which is in Maryland. A majority of the St. Mary's Board of County Commissioners were caught red handed meeting illegally in violation of Maryland law with the chief legal elected official who should have known better.

"The lame ducks are dead ducks now." thought Jarvis as he turned off the computer and went to bed.

At 3:00 A.M., Jarvis got up and drew a very specific schematic diagram of the Largent hydrogen generator with his magic marker on back of an old Lucky Strike Saloon placemat. He wrote down the date on the bottom right hand corner, September 11, 2011. Jarvis opened up Country's guitar case and put the diagram under his guitar. Then he slept till daybreak.

In the morning, they loaded the ElecTrike into the bed of the Dodge truck and Country headed out to Interstate 95 to start work in Richmond.

He dropped Jarvis with his provisions, his guitar, and his electric trike off at the exit to Route 301 South.

Country handed Jarvis his business card.

"Ronald C. Gentry - Lightning Rod Installer" Jarvis read the card aloud. "So, that's your name."

"And, what's your name" asked Country.

"Jarvis" was the reply.

Country drove off, waved, and called out the window, "See you later, Jerry."

"Maybe the boy does know a little, but he won't tell." thought Jerry Largent as he rubbed the ring on his little finger and rolled south.

As the two friends parted in separate directions to start new chapters in their lives, the world was going to close a hundred year chapter of energy technology suppression. There was nothing the Council of 33 could do to stop it.

ABOUT THE AUTHOR

Larry Jarboe regularly penned articles on common sense in government, conservation and clean energy issues for 20 years on a weekly basis in ST. MARY'S TODAY newspaper. He currently writes on a variety of fishing, boating, and travel as well as energy topics in THE CHESAPEAKE and is the editor of the publication.

Elected to the first of four terms in 1994 as a St. Mary's County Commissioner, Larry Jarboe has practiced a conservative Republican philosophy of being frugal with the taxpayer's money and yet has always supported the funding needed for public schools, public safety and vital services while casting a strong no vote on expenditures which are capricious and wasteful.

Larry has been a charter boat captain and operated a saw mill in Charlotte Hall, Maryland for 25 years. He regularly explores new methods in providing clean and affordable energy as well as new fishing holes and methodology in catching fish.

Larry's expertise on luring fish onto his line includes serenades and lullabies along with renewable bait such as grass shrimp. Larry also perfected the art of snorklefishing which was so effective it was outlawed. See more on Larry Jarboe's newest articles and books at **www.the-chesapeake.com**

Made in United States
Orlando, FL
01 April 2023

31639458R00095